Frightening strikes

A fire, a break-in, an horrific car crash: it looked as though fate had it in for high-flying lawyer, aspiring politician and world-class womaniser Claude Chavanac.

But was it fate? Or something more corporeal?

With half of France closed down for the summer vacation, gourmet plod Georges Albuisson, and his insubordinate side-kick Jacques Andrieu, make a few desultory enquiries to while away the time.

There's no shortage of possible suspects: jealous husbands and discarded mistresses, disgruntled clients and vengeful villains, professional rivals and political opponents, even the Hippopotamus . . .

How does the wily old politician fit into the picture? Or the ex-neighbour with his sexy young wife and her ice-blonde predecessor? Old friends from the past, the newlywed couple, the goat-keeping monk?

Or was it just a series of accidents after all? But then, why would someone pull strings with a top-ranking police chief to get the investigation stopped?

A twisted trail leads Albuisson and Andrieu from the Auvergne to Provence, Paris, Brittany and the Chartreuse, but no nearer to the answer – while in a peaceful Provençal village, amid the scents of herbs and garlic and the gentle click of *boules* on the *pétanque* pitch, frightening strikes again.

With a helping hand from Zoe Chavanac, Claude's quick-thinking English wife – and an inadvertent contribution from his own aged mother – Albuisson finally makes the right connection.

Almost.

Also by Hilary Whelan

Dead cow (1994)

FRIGHTENING STRIKES

Hilary Whelan

Constable · London

First published in Great Britain 1995
by Constable & Company Ltd
3 The Lanchesters, 162 Fulham Palace Road
London W6 9ER

ISBN 0 09 474060 7
Set in Linotron Palatino 10pt by
CentraCet Ltd, Cambridge
Printed and bound in Great Britain by
Hartnolls Ltd, Bodmin

A CIP catalogue record for this book
is available from the British Library

Thursday 9th June, Auvergne, France

There's a car, little more than a speck in the distance, speeding across the high plateau. The road is a long, straight line drawn through the lush green of early summer, under a huge blue sky hung with hawks. This is the *planèze*, an empty land of rugged pastures, founded on ancient lava flows from the long-defunct Cantal volcanoes whose weathered cores serrate the horizon ahead.

In the car is Claude Chavanac, heading home from a lunch in the town of St-Flour, which styles itself the capital of the Haute Auvergne. This was a lunch about politics rather than food, a lunch for forging alliances and influencing people. Nevertheless, he has eaten well, and sampled a glass or two of good wine (but not too many, as the blood tests will later show).

He's not as good a driver as he thinks he is, but better than most; he knows his car, he doesn't take unnecessary risks. It's a fast car, and he drives it fast; but not too fast. Zoe, his wife, might disagree – but who is she to talk? Every inch the smart, sharp-thinking, professional woman, yet she drives like a scatterbrained floozie, with a reckless abandon that scares the wits out of him. And this is an Englishwoman, one of a race that misses no opportunity to criticize the driving habits of the French.

But there's no one here to criticize him now. His wife's some seventy kilometres away, collecting the children from school in their home town, St-Geraud; and he's alone with an empty road on a glorious day, and free to drive just as he pleases.

His thoughts swivel back to the lunch he's just left. A success? Hard to tell. Guest of honour was Grand Old Man Albert Brunet: ex-mayor, ex-*député*, ex-minister; a local boy made good in Paris politics – or bad, according to your point of view – and now retired home to rest on his laurels.

Brunet shares his name with one of the loftier peaks of the Cantal – and in some ways, Claude feels, he resembles those ancient volcanoes in whose shadow he was raised: in their younger days, towering and terrible, explosive, sulphurous and lethal; but now reduced and worn down with time, fires extinguished, apparently calm. And yet, not to be underestimated. With age, both man and mountains have acquired a different, less strident kind of grandeur, and an air of mature benevolence that nevertheless only partly conceals a residual potential for danger.

Claude knows why he was invited to this lunch. He has his own political ambitions – purely local, for the time being at least, but who knows . . .? He was being put on show, set up to be given the once-over by the experienced old-timer. What kind of impression did he make? What's the old bastard saying about him, now that he's tactfully departed, leaving the others to talk about him behind his back?

Nothing very complimentary, he's willing to bet. The two of them are chalk and cheese. The old man's crude and earthy, still cultivating his image as a horny-handed son of the soil – though it's decades since those hands have had dirt under their fingernails – while Claude's the city-slick lawyer with his good looks and designer suit, even if in origin and at heart he's as much an Auvergnat as Brunet ever was.

All through the lunch, he could feel Brunet skimming his surface, ticking off his assessment in clichés: too clever, too cool, too calculating.

Too bad. If the old man gives him the thumbs-down, he can live with it. He's not fool enough to ignore Brunet's lingering influence, but he's got time on his side. Right now, Brunet still has the heady aura of Paris about him, but that will fade; before long, he'll be just another has-been in a bar, trading old Mitterrand stories for drinks.

Now the road is curling down towards Murat, little grey town sheltering at the base of a great pudding-shaped lump of basalt, and overlooked by a massive madonna as subtle and dazzlingly white as a detergent commercial. Claude drives through the town and out along the road towards St-Geraud. This road climbs steeply, twisting round the contours, and then he's over the top and gliding easily down into the valley. He passes a truck, pulls back in and gently brakes.

Too gently, it seems. He brakes harder.

He registers, surprisingly calmly, that the brakes are not working. He's rolling at some speed down a sinuous mountain road, and the brakes are not working.

He changes down the gears and pulls on the handbrake. That slows him down a little, but not enough, and leaves him with a nasty smell of burning oil and rubber. But at least he can still control the car around the bends and, thank God, there's no other vehicle in front of him.

He tries to visualize the road ahead: are there turnings he could safely take, tracks where he could bump to a halt in a field? At intervals along these high roads, he knows, there are lay-bys, where heaps of sand and grit are stored in case of the snow and ice that can strike even this late in the year: perhaps if he runs the car into one of those, he thinks, he can stop without too much damage. But where is the next one? Although he knows the road well – he's driven along it hundreds of times – his mind's a blank, and he comes around a bend unable to remember what lies beyond it.

All too quickly, he knows. The road, still descending, unfurls into a long, straight stretch through a village. And, right ahead of him, a tangle of children straggle across it, from the school on one side to the main part of the village, and the waiting school bus, on the other.

This village has gone to some lengths to protect its children: there are warning lights flashing, pedestrian crossings, bumps in the road surface to slow down the traffic; and all of them as effectual as crossed fingers and touched wood against a car with no brakes.

Claude, fending off panic, holds a split-second debate with himself. It seems remarkable how many things he is able to take into consideration in so short a time. The options: steer to the right, into a solid wall of rock; to the left, down a steep and stony bank; or straight ahead, into a mass of children.

When he sounds the horn, they all turn to look, but they seem not to realize what is happening. They're too young to judge the speed of the oncoming car, to understand that it might not be able to stop. Only when it's already too late do they begin to sense danger, and start to scatter.

He thinks of himself, fear of impact, fear of pain, fear of falling, fear of the unknown.

He thinks of his wife.

He thinks of his own children, and the impact of hard metal at high velocity on soft chubby flesh and fragile little bones.

He thinks: Jesus, Mary and Joseph.

Then he says to himself: 'Oh, fuck it!' and swings the wheel to the left.

Four days later, an announcement appears in the Personal section of the small ads in the local newspaper. It says 'C.C. – Here's to the next time.'; but nobody notices it then.

1

Zoe Chavanac slid into the pool and swam its length underwater, barely rippling the polished blue surface. Emerging at the opposite end, she performed a few fast, ferocious lengths of front crawl, throwing up showers of spray to glitter in the sunlight.

Then she decided that was quite enough of that, and climbed out of the pool to lounge in the shade of the umbrella pines that sheltered the corner of the terrace. The water slowly calmed to a gentle sway, reflecting hypnotic ripples of light upon the creamy-white plaster of the poolhouse wall.

Unwilling to summon the energy to walk into the house and find her sun-glasses, she squinted through half-closed eyes against the dazzle of the mid-morning sun, across the rolling hectares of vineyards criss-crossed with cypresses. It was so hot and still she could practically hear the grapes ripening.

Beyond the vines, to the south, lay the Luberon – close to, a massive ridge of steep wooded hills slashed with vicious ravines; but from here, in the haze of the heat, just a long grey shape, like a huge sleeping animal. A good name for it, Zoe thought sleepily: Luberon, looming, lumbering, slumbering . . .

She let herself doze. Everyone else was asleep somewhere, or out doing constructive and interesting things, which to Zoe was not at all the point of a holiday. After the aggravations of the past few months – the car crash, the fire, the break-in (she dearly hoped there was some truth in the superstition that disasters come in threes) – she was devoting herself to peaceful oblivion.

When some ill-defined period of time had ambled past – time being an imprecise and little-regarded commodity in a Provençal August – she stirred at the sound of tyres on gravel. Slowly, she eased herself off the lounger, slipped on her espadrilles – the terrace was too hot for the bare feet of any but the most hardened fire-walker – and strolled to the house.

It was a big, low, ground-hugging place, built of a luminous, honey-coloured stone and roofed with faded terracotta tiles, so that it looked as though it had grown organically out of the pale earth it stood upon. In a sense, it had done exactly that, with bits springing up here and there as need dictated; and now it rambled all over the place, on different levels, with unexpected courtyards and surprising terraces.

Once, it had been a traditional *mas*, home to some extended family who had farmed the fields around for generations; now it was cleaned up and prettified, embellished with pool and gardens, tennis court and *pétanque* pitch, for the well-heeled of colder latitudes to sweat away their summers in.

In the enormous kitchen, with its lumpy, rough-plastered stone walls and aged ceiling beams, its huge open fireplace and rustic hearth, its state-of-the-art, microchip-controlled Neff double oven and microwave, Zoe's sister-in-law stood by the long pine table, unloading purchases from tastefully artisanal straw shopping bags.

'Unbelievable!' she enthused. 'Apt market, absolutely marvellous; I mean, *everything*. All the tourist stuff, lavender whatnots, wonderful fabrics – but then all the down-to-earth local stuff as well. And *real* food. I never knew there were so many kinds of olives. Oh, and the way the stalls go meandering through the old town, in those little narrow streets. You really should have come. Even the buskers are classy; there was this beautiful young man playing a harp.'

'Probably an angel,' said Zoe. Having spent many summers in the area, she was well acquainted with the charms of the Saturday market, but this morning she had declined Moira's insistent invitation to accompany her.

As far as Zoe was concerned, there were two ways of approaching a market: either you went there for practical reasons, to buy things you needed, in which case you set about it in a businesslike manner; or else you went for gentle, leisurely amusement, dawdling along and letting your senses be snatched by the sights and sounds and smells of things enticing or bizarre.

Moira, on the other hand, turned every excursion into a cross between an Everest expedition and a school outing with an extremely earnest teacher. Everything had to be researched, identified, examined, experienced. It was all such bloody hard work.

When she had proposed a visit to the market, everyone had suddenly remembered they had something else to do; only Lucie, Zoe's daughter, had been persuaded to go with her. Lucie, at eight, could still be stirred into enthusiasm by adult-inspired activities – unlike her nine-year-old ('I'm practically ten!') brother Fredy, who was still, Zoe presumed, snoring in his pit somewhere in the depths of the house.

Moira continued to enumerate her acquisitions. 'I got this bolt of cloth. It's a really good glazed cotton. I thought it'd look lovely in Chiara's room. Curtains and a quilt cover, don't you think?'

Zoe nodded, though she wondered if the pretty Provençal print, in its sunny greens and yellows, would have quite the same appeal on a rainy day in Manchester.

Moira went on, and on. 'This little blue frock for Chiara; isn't it sweet? And some of that gorgeous air-dried mountain ham. And a great big pot of basil – smell it!' Difficult not to. 'Goat cheese,' she added. 'Three different kinds.' Also hard to miss. 'Oh, and this,' Moira said, unwrapping a painted pot with a slot in the top.

'What's that for?' asked Zoe.

'It's an English box.' Zoe looked none the wiser. Moira said: 'Like a swear box, only instead of putting money in when you swear, you have to put in a franc every time you speak English.'

'Why?' said Lucie, ingenuously (and in English, since this was what everyone happened to be speaking at the time).

'Because', explained Moira (also in English, and apparently oblivious to irony), 'Uncle Hugo and Chiara and I want to be able to speak French as well as you do, darling, and the only way to learn properly is to talk it all the time. If you give up and start talking English whenever you can't think of the word you want, then you never learn anything. Isn't that right, Zoe?'

Zoe sighed, in what Moira took to be the affirmative. Inviting long-time-no-see big brother Hugo and his family over from England to share the villa this August had seemed an inspired idea; but, at the time, she had not been aware of Moira's transformation.

She remembered Moira as a power-dressed career woman, sharp and cynical and funny. Moira and Hugo had been archetypal dinkies – two fat salaries, no kids, eating out every night at the latest place to be seen in, holidaying several times a year on the most exotic beaches and the most exclusive *pistes*. But fashion had changed: consumption out, caring in; babies became desirable accessories, and Moira and Hugo just had to have one, even though she was over forty and he was well on the downhill slope towards the big five-oh.

At least, that was how Zoe interpreted it when she was feeling ill-disposed towards them. In a more charitable frame of mind, she was prepared to concede that there might be other reasons: the maternal imperative, the sense of biological time running out. But, whatever the cause, the effect had extended far beyond the mere production of little Chiara.

Moira had jettisoned her well-paid job – and with it, or so it seemed to Zoe, all sense of wit and discrimination. She had immersed herself in the study of child-rearing, swallowing whole any number of half-baked theories.

She had bought a sewing machine and recipe books, replaced the minimalist furniture with squashy sofas and the Porsche with a Volvo, given her designer clothes to Oxfam, and taken to gardening and going about in floppy frocks. And, with all the enthusiasm of the convert, she rambled on about it, endlessly. Zoe felt her patience, not known for its resilience, already wearing dangerously thin; and the holiday had only just begun.

She was feigning admiration for an olive-wood bowl for which Moira had paid far too much, as Hugo came dozily wandering into the kitchen, looking dusty, followed shortly afterwards by Fredy.

'Lunch?' said Hugo, tentatively.

'You can't possibly be hungry already,' said Moira.

'Well, it is twelve o'clock.'

'You never eat at twelve o'clock at home.'

'I know, but when in Rome . . .'

'It's too hot to cook,' said Zoe. 'I suppose we could go out.'

'They've got *three* McDonalds in Avignon now,' contributed Fredy, hopefully; but everyone ignored him, as usual, so he put on his baseball cap sideways and went off in search of living creatures to torment.

'We'll have salad,' said Moira. 'There's the ham and the cheese and those wonderful tomatoes. It's all right, I'll do it. It won't take a minute.'

So Zoe left her to it, and went back to lie in the shade.

Georges Albuisson, on his way home from police headquarters in St-Geraud, pulled into the drive of the Chavanac house and brought the car to a halt by the kitchen door. As if by magic, the Chavanac cat materialized on the doorstep, fixing him in its disconcerting, multi-coloured stare, one eye brown and one eye blue.

He let himself in with the spare key that Zoe had given him, picked up the empty bowls from the floor and carried them to the sink. With characteristic fastidiousness, he rinsed them and dried them, refilled them with food and fresh water, and set them on the floor. The cat sniffed them warily and then, satisfied, settled down to eat.

Albuisson wondered, and not for the first time, why he had let himself be talked into this. He was not a particular lover of animals, preferring them, on the whole, lightly grilled and served with a nice *Béarnaise* sauce. And he had never considered himself a close friend of the Chavanacs, although circumstances had thrown them together on a number of occasions.

But Zoe had caught him off-guard, appealing to him to feed the cat and keep an eye on the house while the family was on holiday, as though she had selected him especially out of all the many possible candidates for the task – even though he knew full well that he had only been asked because the house happened to be on his way home, and in any case there was no one else to do it.

The rest of the world – or so it seemed – was on holiday, but Albuisson was immune to the allure of August. There were crowds everywhere, the prices rose with the temperature and in inverse proportion to the quality of the food, and he took little pleasure from lying in the sun; there was also the inescapable fact that his physique no longer lent itself to public exposure in shorts and swimwear.

He preferred to take his holidays at quieter times of the year and in places where it was possible to eat well, and he didn't really object to being left behind to mind the shop while everyone else was away. In fact, he quite enjoyed the peace and quiet, the lack of interruption, the opportunity to get things properly organized without interference. And he didn't really mind being asked to keep the Chavanac cat from starvation, though it had to be said that it looked more than capable of fending for itself.

He let himself out, locking the kitchen door behind him; there was a catflap for the animal to get out when it wanted to. Then he took a tour around the outside of the house, checking the windows and doors. Nothing seemed amiss: shutters secured, doors locked; no unaccountable footprints, disturbed foliage, discarded cigarette butts or other signs of intrusion.

He made sure there were no magazines or advertising leaflets overflowing the mailbox, a certain indicator to any passing miscreant that the occupants were absent – although, in August, even without supporting evidence, the absence of the occupants was a pretty safe bet.

The state of the garden, tangled and overgrown, might have offered a further clue, but this would be misleading; anyone familiar with the neighbourhood would have known that it was always like that. Gardening came low on the Chavanacs' list of priorities.

Albuisson stepped cautiously through the undergrowth; he came upon a tangle of wild raspberry canes, and sampled some of the fruit. Wonderful! A stunning intensity of flavour. He rummaged in his pockets for a plastic bag; he usually had one about his person – ostensibly for the purpose of collecting and sealing items of evidence during an investigation, though in practice, as now, they more often came in handy for storing interesting comestibles encountered unexpectedly.

Glancing around with a slightly guilty air – it was just as well he had chosen to be a policeman; he would have made a lousy criminal – he quickly stripped the canes of their fruit. Well, there was no harm in it, was there? No point in letting them go to waste.

Sealing the bag and carrying it casually, whistling a nonchalant air, he came back around the corner of the house towards the kitchen. The wall was charred from the fire, and there was still that faint smell of burnt wood, cinders and ash. Very strange, that, the woodpile just bursting into flames for no apparent reason. Lucky, perhaps, that it was summer, and the pile was depleted. A winter woodpile, if the whole thing caught alight, could have made quite a conflagration.

It had been bad enough as it was, breaking out in the middle of the night; all the logs burning, as well as the shelter that kept them dry, threatening the house and the garage – what if the cars with their full petrol tanks had caught alight, and the oily rags and cans of old paint, jars of white spirit and all the other inflammable garbage that people keep in their garages? And all this while the family were asleep inside the house. It was the cat that had awoken them in time to call the fire brigade before anything disastrous happened; perhaps that was why Zoe was so concerned for its welfare.

The fire brigade had investigated, but declared themselves mystified as to the cause. No trace of any incendiary agent had been found, and there had been no lightning or other strange meteorological phenomena that night. They were at a loss to explain how an innocent woodpile might suddenly immolate itself, but advised that these things do happen. A casually discarded match, an accidental spark, embers thrown out before they were quite dead, heat given off by decomposing vegetable matter – any of these things, normally harmless, had been known, in the right circumstances, to initiate fires.

Albuisson, no expert on these matters, had no strong views either way. Being of a naturally suspicious frame of mind, though, he took a look around each time he visited the house, just in case he should come upon anything unusual. But so far he never had.

Satisfied that all was well for the moment at least, he reached into his pocket for his car keys, preparing to make his way home to Madame Albuisson and something delicious to eat.

And then he caught sight of something which just might have

been the round brown cap of a mushroom, among the underbrush at the foot of a young pine tree a few metres from the house. He paused to investigate and saw that it was indeed a rather fine *cèpe* – and so early in the season! – with a smaller one beside it. He stooped to pick them but, as he did so, his car keys fell to the ground. Cursing mildly, he scrabbled in the grass for them.

The sunlight caught on something metallic and shiny, and he reached for it. But it wasn't the keys. It was a cigarette lighter – the disposable kind, red plastic with a metal cap. He could see through the translucent plastic that the lighter was almost, but not quite, empty.

He studied it for a moment. Whose lighter? He knew Claude Chavanac didn't smoke, and he didn't think Zoe did, either. But that didn't necessarily mean anything. They must have friends who were smokers. And even non-smokers would use lighters sometimes, for other things – lighting barbecues, bonfires, gas burners . . . wood fires?

Maybe.

The thing to do was to put the lighter in the plastic evidence bag, and take it away for forensic examination; but the bag was full of raspberries now, so he wrapped the lighter in his handkerchief and dropped it into his pocket. He reached down again and found his keys, and set off towards the car. When he got home, he realized with annoyance that he'd quite forgotten to pick the *cèpes*.

2

'Enchanting!' gushed the Hippopotamus.

Not the real thing, of course; that was just the nickname that Fredy had given her, and unfortunately it had stuck. She was an immense, orange-clad Parisienne, from what Moira referred to as 'next door', even though the villa the woman was renting was at least a kilometre away.

Moira had made a point of introducing herself to all the neighbours: the 'locals', she called them. Most of them were no more local than she was – they were summer visitors, too, a motley multinational crew – but nevertheless she persisted in behaving like an incomer to Ambridge ingratiating herself with the Archers.

She had taken to inviting little throngs of neighbours for aperitifs at midday. This was all very well with the French and the Belgians, who, after a drink or two, scuttled off to eat; but other nationalities often failed to appreciate the seminal significance of lunch, and had a nasty habit of hanging around all day.

'Quite enchanting,' cried the Hippopotamus, again. She was gazing down upon Chiara, who was indeed looking rather appealing, with her new blue Provençal print dress and her slightly fey expression. You always had the faint suspicion that Chiara might be from another galaxy, a foundling smuggled into the human race by some other species which wishes us no harm but finds us just a trifle perplexing.

'What's she called?' enquired Madame P, one of the few true locals in attendance. Madame P – no one seemed to know what the P stood for – ran the *alimentation générale* in the nearby village. As the sole source of provisions in the neighbourhood, this made Madame P a person of some consequence.

'Chiara,' Moira told her. Madame P frowned. 'It's Italian,' Moira said.

Madame P looked puzzled. 'Your child is Italian?'

'No, no – English, like us. We were in Tuscany the summer before she was born,' Moira added, as though this explained everything. 'It's such a pretty name, don't you think?'

Madame P grunted. She was of the general opinion that English children should be given English names, French children French names, and so on. But the Hippopotamus beamed radiantly.

'Charming,' she said. She was well into her fourth or fifth *pastis*. Madame P grunted again, and stomped away in search of someone sensible to talk to.

Chiara, bored, waited until no one was looking and then scuttled off to the swimming pool. An only child, with few friends of her own age, she was accustomed to the company of grown-ups, but still found them bewildering and slightly frightening, especially *en masse* and with drinks in their hands. She escaped when she could from the forest of thighs and bottoms, exaggerated gestures and loud voices, to the more benign universe of things on her own level: bushes, grass, flowers, low walls and small creatures.

The cat was at the edge of the pool, down by the deep end. She'd seen it there before. It was a thin scrap of a thing, not much more than a kitten, that lived half-wild and half off the indulgence of visitors. It came to the swimming pool to drink, not deterred by the chlorine in the water.

The pool had a stone surround with an overhanging lip, and the water lay some distance below. In order to drink, the cat had to perch precariously over the rim, in clear contravention of the laws of gravity. Chiara was impressed. She crouched down alongside the cat, imitating its stance, to see how it was done.

Zoe, stepping out on to the terrace at just that moment, suppressed the instinct to cry out, for fear of making matters worse. Instead, with a sharp intake of breath, she moved stealthily towards the pool, swooped down and swept the little girl up in her arms.

Chiara howled in protest. The cat fled. Zoe heard footsteps and turned to see Moira approaching, looking quite unconcerned. She put Chiara down, and started gently to explain to her the perils of the swimming pool.

'There's no need to worry,' Moira said nonchalantly. 'She learnt to swim before she could walk – all the experts say it's the best way, before they're old enough to develop a fear of water.'

Zoe looked surprised. 'But she never goes in the pool.'

'Well, no,' Moira conceded. 'She doesn't actually seem to *like* it very much. But the important thing is that she's not at all afraid. She swims like a little dolphin.'

Blowing water out of the top of her head, presumably, thought Zoe intemperately; or is that whales? She watched Chiara running off through a thicket of rosemary bushes in pursuit of the cat, and felt an inclination to follow her, to escape the tedious necessity of being polite to the neighbours.

There was quite a collection here today. Apart from Madame P, and the Hippopotamus – accompanied everywhere by a tiny young man (Moira had suggested that he was her toyboy, Hugo that he was her lunch) – there was a family of large Germans, a terribly refined Swiss couple and a trio of Dutch equestrians who went everywhere on horseback and had parked their mounts in the drive alongside the cars.

Then there was a young couple who rode a motor bike and hardly spoke to anyone and were generally known as the Newlyweds, a jolly pair of pensioners from Orléans, and two self-conscious young men from Suffolk who had taken offence when Hugo asked if they were familiar with the tyre shop in Cavaillon that went by the name of Gay Pneus.

Zoe attached herself to the pensioners. They were cheerfully dissecting the foibles of their fellow guests.

'I don't know, kids!' the wife was saying, gesturing towards the female Newlywed. 'No sense of style. Such a pretty girl, she could look lovely if she tried.'

The girl was all in black: clinging halter-neck vest, leather waistcoat, cycling shorts and heavy black laced shoes. Her hair was cut very short, almost a crew-cut; her only adornments were a pair of chunky silver ear-rings, a man-sized watch and a gash of lipstick the colour of dried blood.

'You're out of touch, my dear,' said the husband. 'She *is* trying. They all look like that, it's the fashion today.'

'But it's so ugly. Those shoes . . .'

'Young 'uns always have funny ideas about clothes. We wore some pretty odd things in our time. Remember those yellow trousers of mine?' They both convulsed at the thought. 'Anyway,' the old man said, '*he* doesn't seem to mind.' He nodded in the direction of the male Newlywed, who was gazing fondly down upon the girl.

'I can remember when you used to look at me like that,' said the old lady, flirtatiously.

'So can I, love – but, unfortunately, I can't remember why.'

Zoe laughed with them, and tried to recall whether Claude had ever looked at her like that. Perhaps not. Fondness had never been his most striking attribute.

The Swiss couple came along. 'We just wanted to tell you', the woman said, earnestly, 'that we read all about your husband in the papers, and we thought what he did was so heroic, sacrificing his own safety for the sake of all those children. You must be so proud of him.'

'What did he do?' said the old man, curious.

'Oh, you must have read about it,' the Swiss woman said. 'It was in all the papers, even at home.'

'We never read the papers. Too depressing. When you get to our age, life's too short to be depressed.'

Undaunted, the Swiss woman relayed the story of Claude's car crash, in all its grisly detail.

'Oh, dear,' said the old man, sadly.

'And I don't believe they ever established exactly what made the brakes fail, did they?' the woman asked Zoe. 'I read that – '

But what she had read remained unreported, as Lucie came running up excitedly, with one of the German children.

'Mummy!' she cried. 'The horses have got loose and they're eating the geraniums.'

'And one of them,' said the German child, solemnly, 'has crapped on the *pétanque* pitch.'

Everyone hurried back through the house to watch the spectacle of the Dutch in pursuit of their horses, the Germans trying to help and the Hippopotamus shouting encouragement from the sidelines. By now, with even more *pastis* inside her, she was swaying precariously; but, being constructed on similar lines to the type of toy with a weighted bottom, which cannot be made to fall over, she remained disappointingly upright. Madame P, meanwhile, scanned the *pétanque* pitch with an entrepreneurial eye. You could get good money for horse manure.

The eventual recapture of the horses was met with a resounding cheer; but after that a sense of anticlimax fell upon the gathering, and people starting saying polite goodbyes and making their way to their cars. The elderly couple sought out Zoe, as she inspected the remains of the geraniums.

'My dear, I hope you don't think we were insensitive,' said the old man, kindly. 'We hadn't heard about your husband's accident. Please accept our sympathy.'

'That's very sweet of you,' said Zoe, with a smile. 'But there's no need to apologize. Claude's not deceased; he just can't stand parties.'

*

'Dead, isn't it?'

'What is?' said Albuisson, only half-listening, trying to concentrate on the report he was reading.

'This place.' Jacques Andrieu waved his hand around the office. 'August's always dead. Nothing ever happens.'

This was not entirely true. All around St-Geraud, villains were breaking into empty houses and nicking things, tourists were having their cars broken into and their pockets picked, and hot August nights provoked outbreaks of violence in some of the less-favoured districts of the town.

But most of the break-ins would not be discovered until the owners returned from their vacations, and the rest was petty stuff which hardly merited the attentions of the Police Judiciaire. Serious crime was thin on the ground. Ongoing investigations were pursued in a desultory way, but even these often ground to a halt, because all the lawyers were on holiday too.

'What you reading?' Andrieu said. Somehow, despite his years of training and experience, the concept of proper hierarchical behaviour seemed to have escaped him; he spoke to everyone, even his elders and superiors, in the same matey manner. One of these days, it was going to get him into serious trouble.

But not today; Albuisson felt far too lazy to protest. He said: 'It's the report on Claude Chavanac's car crash.'

Andrieu frowned. 'Accident, wasn't it?'

'So they say.'

Albuisson debated: would it be a good idea to tell Andrieu what was on his mind? It wasn't official business – just idle curiosity, really, and not to be taken seriously. But if Andrieu was bored, it might give him something to think about. In Albuisson's experience, a bored young policeman with nothing to do could be a liability.

Andrieu was twenty-seven; he was bright and his prospects were good. But he had, to Albuisson's mind, a rather over-Americanised view of life – a vision of cruising the streets in a low-slung performance car, living off burgers and beers in diners, inviting punks to make his day. St-Geraud was, fortunately, not the kind of town that lent itself readily to such behaviour, but, all the same . . .

What Andrieu needed, Albuisson felt, was a sensible wife and a couple of kids, but as yet there seemed little prospect of that. Hence his presence here in August, when preference on the holiday rota was given to family men with school-age children.

Now he was peering over Albuisson's shoulder. 'You think there might have been more to the crash than meets the eye?'

Albuisson shrugged. He was not a man to rush to conclusions.

'I suppose', said Andrieu, 'there was that other business, wasn't there? The fire at Chavanac's house, I mean.'

'There was also a break-in at his apartment in St-Geraud.'

'Oh, yes. I remember hearing about that. Vandals, wasn't it? Made a mess, but didn't steal anything.'

'So it would appear.'

'And you think the three things might have been connected? Someone who's got it in for Chavanac, for some reason?'

'Well, yes, I had been wondering. Although . . .' Albuisson pondered. 'The fire and the break-in, they could have been vindictive; intended to cause trouble but not really dangerous. But engineering a car crash that could have been fatal – that's something else altogether. Who'd have it in for Chavanac badly enough to do something like that?'

Andrieu said: 'Are you kidding? I can think of a hundred people.'

'Like who?'

'Well, the husbands of most of the good-looking women in St-Geraud, for a start.' Claude Chavanac's philandering was legendary.

'I don't know,' said Albuisson. 'They seem to take a fatalistic view of it – they know they're in good company. In fact, I think they feel insulted if they're left out; it suggests their wives aren't good enough.'

'Well, what about the women themselves, then? An old flame who resented being dumped?'

'From what I've heard, most of the ladies are still well disposed towards him, even when he's moved on to the next. I don't know what he's got, but they seem to like it.'

Andrieu laughed. 'You mean apart from looks, charm, wit, lots of money and a dong the size of a donkey's?'

'Is it?' said Albuisson, in all seriousness.

'I haven't the faintest idea, but I wouldn't be at all surprised. It would explain a lot.'

'I'm not sure that most women care about that kind of thing quite as much as most men imagine they do.'

'It would be nice to think so,' said Andrieu, a trifle wistfully.

'Anyway, he's supposed to be a reformed character these days. They say he got a nasty shock when his wife threw him out last year, and since they got back together again, he's been as good as gold.'

Andrieu nodded understandingly. 'I could never figure out why, with a classy wife like that, he bothered chasing women in the first place. Mind you, she looks like she might be a bit of a ball-breaker, don't you think?'

If Albuisson had an opinion on the subject, he was not prepared to divulge it to a subordinate. He said, reflectively: 'I suppose, despite what I said before, it *is* possible that a cuckolded husband might have had a grievance against Chavanac – doesn't have to be recent, does it? Could be dating back years. A woman, though – I don't know; would a woman tamper with a car's brakes? Would she know how?' Albuisson had a somewhat old-fashioned notion of women.

'I'm not sure *I*'d know how,' said Andrieu. 'Did the accident investigators find any signs that the brakes had been got at?'

'They couldn't say for certain that they had; but, reading the report again, I can't see anything to convince me that they hadn't. It says there may have been a leakage of fluid that could have resulted in brake failure, but the relevant bits of the car were too badly damaged for anyone to be certain what caused it.'

'What about the car's service history?'

'It was fairly new – less than six months old; only had about five thousand kilometres on the clock. Chavanac had it serviced at Combelle's garage – you know, the one by the roundabout? They're no cowboys. Their mechanics are well qualified, and they don't cut corners; they've got a good reputation and they want to keep it. According to their records, they had the car in on the Monday before the accident, and the brakes were all right then. And Chavanac said this was the first time he'd used it since, apart from driving it home from the garage.'

'Could somebody have got at one of the mechanics, maybe?'

'It doesn't look as if anybody bothered to investigate. No reason why they should, if they thought it was an accident.'

'I could check it out, if you like. I've not got much else to do.'

'All right,' said Albuisson. 'You check it out.'

3

From the privacy of a shady roof terrace, Claude watched the round-up of the horses with mild amusement. An aversion to parties was not quite the whole story; he found them tolerable if there were interesting women about and he was free to circulate at his leisure – but, in the current circumstances, neither condition was satisfied.

Lack of mobility, that was the worst part. He'd been lucky, no doubt about that; most of the damage from the crash had been fairly superficial and long since healed, leaving nothing to show except a rather dashing scar above one eyebrow. But his right leg had been badly mangled and had to be put back together with steel pins and plastic – and bits of string and sealing wax, for all he knew. The surgeons assured him he'd be fine, eventually, apart from perhaps a slight limp which would not inconvenience him greatly; but full recovery was going to take some time.

He could stand unsupported now, but not for long. And, although he could get about quite well with the aid of crutches, it required superhuman dexterity to do so while at the same time holding both a glass and a conversation.

There was a wheelchair, but he hated using it; it made him feel a hundred years old. People would stand around him and talk over his head, as though he were invisible, and ask each other whether he would like a drink. And the only other option – to park himself somewhere while the party ebbed and flowed around him, and the most boring person in the room latched upon him like a limpet – somehow lacked appeal.

As for interesting women, well, Claude was a faithful husband these days. Not that he had much choice in the matter, in his present state of health. But even before the accident, he had drastically curtailed his adventuring – and it had turned out to be less of a loss than he had imagined. A sign of the times, he supposed: age and circumstances; one had to be more careful nowadays. And if good sex was all he wanted, he could get that at home. The effect of the crash had rather cramped his style, but Zoe had come up with some quite unmatronly innovations that left him wondering where she'd learned them, but reluctant to enquire for fear that he might not like the answer.

He still found it difficult, though, to resist the frisson of a mild flirtation, even if it led to nothing. In truth, that had always been the main attraction. He had friends who were ardent hunters; he had never shared their passion, but he recognized that some of the sensations were similar. Like them, he preferred the pace of the chase to the thrill of the kill – and the aftermath was often disappointing.

Today, though, there was nothing of interest to pursue. The German women were good-looking, but too big and bossy. The dark-haired girl was pretty, but very young, and he had always felt it slightly unsporting to make a play for a new bride. The rest were too old, too fat or too ridiculous. On the whole, he was better off where he was.

'Any luck with the garage mechanics?' said Albuisson.

Andrieu shook his head. 'Nah. Pure as the driven snow, the lot of them. None of them on police files, and the owner let me see their personnel records; they all look perfectly respectable, good references. And no connection with Chavanac, apart from working on his car.'

'What about money? Could someone have paid them to do it?'

'They're pretty well-paid, and none of them had money problems, as far as I could tell. And if someone was paying, they'd have had to have bought at least two of these guys, if not more. Everyone I spoke to agreed that, the last time they had the car in there, none of them was ever alone with it at any time. There were always at least two people working on it.'

'Even during the lunch break?'

'They were busy that day; worked right through lunch.' Albuisson looked incredulous. 'It's true,' Andrieu assured him. 'I checked all the documentation – their time log, the worksheet for the car, the work report they gave to Chavanac – and it didn't look as if they could have fiddled it.'

Albuisson scowled. One greedy, dishonest, potentially murderous mechanic: possibly. But two, three?

'You want me to check their bank accounts?' said Andrieu.

'We'd never get authorization – insufficient grounds for suspicion.'

'There are other ways . . .'

'No,' said Albuisson, firmly. 'Drop it. The whole thing's probably nothing more than a set of coincidences.'

But Andrieu, once switched on, was not so easily turned off. He said: 'I'm not sure. That break-in at Chavanac's apartment: I read through the file and had a look at the photographs. Now, on the surface, it's just vandalism – stuff thrown about, paint on the walls, et cetera. But there was very little permanent damage. There was glassware there, china, mirrors, ornaments – and none of it was broken. That doesn't seem right. I've seen a fair bit of vandalism in my time, and they're not usually that careful. Fragile stuff gets smashed. And even if they're not out to steal, if they're just doing it for the hell of it, they almost always take something, small things they can put in their pockets, at least. But there was money on the dressing-table, solid gold cufflinks, a cheque-book, a watch, a Mont Blanc pen, just sitting there asking to be lifted – and yet they didn't take any of it.'

'Yes, that does seem odd,' admitted Albuisson.

'But the oddest thing', said Andrieu, 'is that the only really serious, permanent damage was to some dusty old law books.'

'Law books?'

'Apparently, Chavanac collects them, and he kept some of them at the apartment. They were all very rare and quite valuable; virtually irreplaceable. And they'd been ripped to shreds – pages torn out, ink poured over them, bindings slashed with a knife. Now, that doesn't sound to me like random vandalism. That sounds deliberate – and done by someone who must have known Chavanac well enough to know that he cared about those books; the rest was just a cover to make it look like vandalism.'

Now, why didn't I think of that? thought Albuisson.

At breakfast, Sunday morning, Moira said: 'I think there's something in the roof.'

'What sort of something?' said Zoe.

'Some kind of animal, I suspect. I woke up in the middle of the night and heard these noises.'

'You have to expect that sort of thing in these old farmhouses,' said Claude. 'It's probably just mice.'

'No, it sounded bigger than that.'

'Cats?' suggested Zoe.

'I don't think so. They're very soft-footed. This was more sort of, I don't know . . . scratchy.'

'Rats!' said Fredy, gleefully. 'Great big horrible hairy rats.'

Lucie shuddered. 'Stop it,' Zoe told him. 'You'll have her awake all night – and Chiara.' And me too, probably, she thought.

'All right,' said Fredy. 'Hamsters, then.'

Lucie giggled. 'That's silly,' she said.

'*Giant* hamsters,' said Fredy, warming to his theme. He puffed out his cheeks and made squeaking noises, and the pair of them fell about in convulsions.

'Well, I think someone ought to have a look up there,' said Moira. 'Whatever it is, it might be gnawing through the power cables or something.'

'Don't look at me,' said Claude, so she looked at Hugo instead.

'I haven't the faintest idea how you get into the roof-space,' he said. 'But there's that caretaker chap that comes round every few days to check the pool filters and the bottled gas and what-not. He'll be here again tomorrow; we can ask him then.'

Slightly mollified, Moira got up to clear the dishes. 'Can't hang around here all day,' she said. 'It's practically time for lunch.'

Claude had booked a table at the restaurant in the village. The women and children opted to walk there, in the interests of working up an appetite, but it was too far for Claude, so he and Hugo were to follow on later by car.

It was a pretty village, but not self-consciously so; nobody had set out to make it like that, it just was: a heap of old buildings on the side of a hill, so that from a distance it was sometimes hard to tell if you were looking at a man-made artefact or a natural outcrop of rock. Close up, you saw steep and narrow cobbled streets with sudden twists and turns, walls of light-reflecting stone, doors and shutters painted dusty blue, and brilliant flowers billowing from windowsills.

'Isn't this just the essence of Provence!' declared Moira, rapt, but no one was listening. Chiara was chatting to a cat that lay basking on a doorstep. Zoe had gone into Madame P's shop to buy a newspaper, and Fredy and Lucie had discovered an enormous toad beneath the fountain in front of the Mairie. It sat squatly in the shade, watching them crossly with bright red eyes.

'Absolutely not,' said Zoe, arriving just as Fredy was about to ask if he could take it home.

'It could live under the kitchen sink and catch flies,' he suggested.

'It might be an improvement on that foul-smelling fly spray,' said Moira.

'Don't encourage him,' Zoe said.

Moira said, earnestly: 'One should never stifle a child's initiative.'

'Where did you read that?' said Zoe. Realizing with alarm that Moira was about to tell her, at some length, she added quickly: 'Come on, let's walk up to the top.'

The children scrambled ahead, up a steep winding alley that opened out, finally, into a natural balcony of rock, rimmed with a low dry-stone wall. Below lay the roofs of the village, and beyond that a tapestry of orchards, fields and vineyards, and waves of wooded hills rolling south towards the Luberon.

Moira scrutinized the ramshackle pattern of the roofs, with their ridges of tiles in faded shades of pink and grey and ochre. 'What are those for?' she asked, pointing at the rows of large, flattish rocks laid apparently haphazardly upon the tiles, along the exposed edges of the roofs.

'They're to hold down the tiles in the *mistral,*' Zoe told her. 'The wind's so strong sometimes, it literally raises the roof.'

Moira frowned. 'Looks dangerous to me. Those rocks must be dreadfully heavy, and they're just perched there any old how, not cemented on or anything. Don't they ever fall off?'

'Not to my knowledge.'

Fredy was surveying the landscape with a small telescope, a prized possession that went with him everywhere, along with his Laguiole knife, his compass, string, chewing gum, tradable *pin's* and other essential items.

'You can see our villa from here,' he said.

'Where, where?' demanded Lucie.

'There.' He pointed to the south-east; there was a clump of trees surrounded by vineyards, and through a dip in the trees a building was partly visible.

'Let's have a look,' said Zoe. She focused the telescope and saw the villa come into vision: the north-facing side, with its terrace that offered welcome shade in the heat of the day.

'Can you see Daddy?' asked Lucie; Claude regularly installed himself there, with a book and a tall glass of something cold and mildly alcoholic.

'I should hope not,' said Moira, severely, checking her watch. 'He and Hugo ought to be on their way to the restaurant by now.'

They walked back down through the village, stopping at intervals to divert Chiara from ambient distractions – cats and dogs, butterflies, empty snail shells and absolutely anything smelly or sticky, the more revolting the better. As they came towards the restaurant, they saw Hugo striding up the hill towards them, looking vaguely disoriented; but this was not unusual for Hugo.

Moira hailed him cheerily. 'Hello, darling. What have you done with Claude?'

'Ah,' said Hugo, awkwardly.

'Ah, what?' said Zoe.

'Well, we went into the restaurant,' he explained, 'and they said they didn't have a table for us. They claimed that Claude had phoned to cancel our reservation, and they'd given our table to someone else. He said he'd done no such thing; they insisted that he had – that he'd said we couldn't come because there'd been a death in the family, of all things. He said they must have been mistaken, it was someone else who'd cancelled and they'd got the names mixed up; they said no, it was definitely Chavanac. So then he said . . . well, I'm not sure precisely *what* he said, actually; my comprehension of vulgar French isn't quite that advanced. But anyway, at this point they got very agitated, and I thought it might be best if we left.'

'Bloody Claude,' said Zoe. 'Soul of tact and diplomacy.'

The professional Claude was smooth as silk, but off duty the sharp edges showed; he was particularly impatient in the face of any apparent inefficiency, stupidity or thoughtlessness, which did not always endear him to those engaged in the service sector. As the party came down the hill, they could see him sitting on a wall, looking thunderous.

'Listen, why don't you lot go in the café and order up some aperitifs,' Zoe suggested. 'I'll go talk to the people in the restaurant and see if I can smooth their ruffled feathers and persuade them to find us a table.' She took Chiara by the hand, saying to Hugo: 'You don't mind if I borrow your winsome child, do you? After Claude's had a go at them, I'll need all the help I can get.'

4

It was Zoe's job to cycle to the village for the breakfast *croissants* and *baguettes*, but Hugo was up early and came along for the ride. They had found a pair of elderly bikes in one of the villa's outbuildings: heavy old butcher's-boy models. Fredy – whose own bike boasted enough gears and gizmos to support an entire Tour de France team – viewed them with contempt; but Zoe was rather fond of them. They were staid and raised no expectations of energetic pedalling.

At this time of day it was almost cool. 'Glorious morning,' said Hugo.

Zoe said nothing. She liked the silence, the lazy journey towards the village on an empty road meandering through deserted vineyards. The roadside verges were full of chicory in flower, unearthly blue like a scattering of fallen sky.

Despite the early hour, Madame P's tiny shop was crowded. Awaiting her turn, Zoe amused herself by counting the number of different products on the shelves. There were hundreds, all jumbled up together: breakfast cereal, sticking plasters, a child's doll; a bottle of twelve-year-old malt whisky and a tin of Swedish meatballs. It was like a magic toyshop; and, with some mysterious sixth sense, Madame P seemed to know exactly where everything was.

On the count of two hundred and three, Zoe became conscious that someone was talking to her. She stopped counting and heard the man ahead of her in the queue saying: 'You don't remember me, do you?'

She blinked, and looked him up and down. 'I'm afraid not. Sorry.'

'That's all right. People never do. It's the hair.' She glanced upwards. 'That's to say,' he said, 'the lack of it.'

He was tall and thin, fortyish, with a shiny, sunburned dome and – as if by way of compensation for the lack of hair on top – a lustrous, bushy brown moustache like a small bear hibernating on his upper lip.

The young woman beside him, all bright red hair and lip-liner and billowing bosoms, giggled and said: 'They always say bald men make the best lovers.'

He grinned and patted her rear proprietorially. 'Number forty-two,' he said.

Unsure of the context, Zoe thought it best to say nothing.

'In the sixteenth,' he added.

Light dawned at last.

'Must be, what . . . ten, eleven years ago?' he said.

Now she could picture him, younger and hairier, met in passing in the hallway, at a party in someone else's flat, borrowing a candle in a power cut. It was Paris; she and Claude had an apartment in a building in the sixteenth *arrondissement*, and he lived on the floor below. And, yes, the number of the building was forty-two – she'd quite forgotten that.

'You've got a better memory than I have,' she said, trying to remember his name.

'Philippe Rocard,' he volunteered, helpfully. 'And this is my wife, Joelle. Jo-Jo, this is Madame Zoe Chavanac. We used to be neighbours, back in Paris.'

'Well, what a coincidence,' said Joelle, as they all shook hands; and then it was her turn to be served.

Andrieu strode down the long dark corridor between the empty offices of the lawyers. Off sunning themselves, he thought; all right for some. At times he resented being stuck with the August shift, wished he was on a beach somewhere, but then he thought of the trip he was planning for the autumn, and that cheered him up. New York, New York! Better than any lousy beach.

Chavanac's office was right at the end of the corridor. He pushed the door – not locked – and went inside. There was a young woman, sitting at a table piled with papers, who looked up in surprise as he came in.

'Sorry,' he said. 'Didn't mean to startle you.'

'I didn't think there was anyone else around.' She pulled a stack of papers together and banged them on the table top to align them, a sharp crack that echoed like a shot in the empty room. 'This place is like a morgue,' she said.

'Right,' said Andrieu. 'In fact, I wasn't expecting to find anybody here.'

'We can't all afford a whole month's holiday,' she said, rather sourly. 'Anyway, this is the best time to get all the files sorted out, when everyone's out of the way. What do you want?'

Andrieu flashed his ID and explained his business.

She frowned suspiciously. 'You got official authority for this?'

'Yes, of course,' he said, not entirely truthfully. 'I'm working for Georges Albuisson.'

'Oh, him.'

She didn't seem impressed. She had a rather cross face that suggested there was little that would impress her. All the same, he caught himself glancing at her hand to see if she was wearing a wedding ring; he seemed to be doing a lot of that these days.

'What do you want to know, then?' she said.

'Are you Chavanac's regular secretary?' She nodded. 'Ever had any trouble with people having a go at him – arguments, nasty letters, rude phone calls?'

She thought about it. 'Not really. There's the odd abusive phone call – you know: relatives of villains who've been sent down, victims who won't accept a decision not to prosecute, that sort of thing. But that's an occupational hazard, par for the course. There's never been anything really nasty, not that I know of. I've overheard a few slanging matches in my time, but that's just business – or domestic.'

'You mean he has rows with his wife?'

'They have the occasional difference of opinion.'

'Are there ever calls from other women?'

'Bits on the side, you mean?' she said, with a hint of disdain, and he wondered for a moment whether she had ever been one of them. Not attractive enough, probably, he thought; but perhaps she would have liked to be. She said: 'To my knowledge, the only affairs he conducts from here are strictly business. And he's not the kind of boss who'd expect his secretary to phone up his wife and make excuses for him, or send roses to his mistresses, or anything like that.'

'Would you do it if he did?'

'Not bloody likely.'

He grinned. 'Can I have a look in his office?'

'If you like, but there's not much to see.'

She walked to the door and swiped her ID card through the electronic lock. Beyond the door, the inner office was bare and tidy: desk, chairs, reading lamps, a bookcase full of legal tomes.

'See what I mean,' she said. 'He doesn't like clutter.'

'What's this, then?' He picked up a little pile of papers from the windowsill. Old newspapers. He blew dust off the top.

'Oh, those,' the secretary said. 'I don't know, really. They came in the post one day, out of the blue. No idea who sent them. There was no note or anything.'

There were three of them, copies of the local paper, *La Montagne*. Different dates, not consecutive, all from the past few months. Andrieu ran his eye swiftly down the front-page headlines, looking for some common factor, but nothing caught his attention.

'I don't suppose you kept the envelope they came in?' he said.

'No. I did have a look at it, though, at the time, to see if there was a return address on the back, or anything to show where it came from, but there wasn't. It had a typed address label, and a St-Geraud postmark.

'When did it arrive?' he said.

'Two or three weeks ago. I can't remember exactly. Why, do you think it's important?'

'Probably not, but you never know. Did Chavanac see these papers?'

'Yes, he was here when they arrived. He'd been coming into the office for the odd day – not taking on new cases, of course, just clearing up some of the old paperwork.'

'Who took over his cases after the accident?' he said. He'd had a vague notion that one of Chavanac's colleagues might have wanted him out of the way. Since the murder case that hit the headlines the year before, Chavanac had been riding a high; he got all the publicity, all the most interesting cases. Someone might have been jealous.

But the girl said: 'No one in particular. They just got farmed out to anyone who had spare capacity.'

'No volunteers?'

'No. There was nothing very exciting on at the time – not the kind of cases that people fight over.'

Forget that idea, then.

He said: 'Did Chavanac have anything to say about these newspapers?'

'He was as much in the dark as I was. We looked through them to see if there were stories that had anything to do with him – like court reports or whatever – but we couldn't see any. He said he was going to take them home and go through them in more detail, but he must have forgotten. I thought I'd better leave them here until he gets back.'

'Oh, well,' he said. 'I think I might take them with me, have a better look at them, if that's all right with you.'

'Please yourself,' she said.

'Just a bunch of kids,' reported Hugo, 'playing in the orchard.'

Moira, hearing noises, had sent him to investigate. They were dining outdoors tonight, watching the picture-book village of Gordes on a distant hillside, as it slowly turned into a cardboard cut-out against a gold and turquoise sunset. Hugo resumed his place at the table, and poured more wine into his glass.

'This is the life,' he said.

Zoe said to Claude: 'I forgot to tell you: guess who Hugo and I ran into in Madame P's this morning?'

'Elvis?' Claude suggested, frivolously.

'No, Philippe Rocard.'

'Who?'

'You know: the chap who used to live downstairs, in Paris . . .'

'Oh. Yes.' Claude's smile faded very slightly, but in the growing twilight no one noticed.

'I didn't recognize him at first,' Zoe said. 'He's got a lot less hair, and a different wife.'

'Really?'

'Yes. The one he had in Paris was our sort of age, if I remember rightly – and blonde, quite elegant. This one's a redhead, much younger.'

'Uncle Hugo said she was a bin-bag,' said Lucie, who had overheard a remark made to Zoe, and been wondering all day what it might mean.

Hugo laughed. 'No, sweetheart, I said she was a bimbo.'

Fredy sniggered.

'Really, Hugo!' said Moira.

'Well, she was,' protested Hugo. 'She was pouting. Anyone who pouts in public at that time of the morning deserves to be called a bimbo.'

'What's a bimbo?' said Lucie.

Meanwhile, in her room, Chiara lay in her little bed under the eaves, trying very hard to stay awake. She was concentrating on the ceiling and listening intently, waiting for the giant hamster to arrive.

At lunchtime, having made sure that Albuisson was not around to see it, Andrieu ducked out for a hamburger and fries, and succumbed to a doughnut as well. Carting them back to his desk in a paper bag, he laid out the three newspapers in front of him and worked his way through them as he munched on the burger.

There was the usual mix of regional and local stories, pictures of *boules* teams and wedding groups, gangs of perky pensioners doing interesting things, and the odd bit of national and global news tucked in at the back. But nothing that seemed to have anything to do with Claude Chavanac.

Nor was there anything to link the separate newspapers – no common thread, no unfolding story running through the three of them. Only one topic appeared in all of them, the ongoing saga of a dust-up in Brussels between Britain, France and Germany; but that had been rumbling right through the summer – nothing special about these three particular days – and it had no conceivable connection with Chavanac.

Andrieu scooped up a last mouthful of salty *frites* and examined the dates on the mastheads. Were they all the same day of the week, the same date in the month, a regular distance apart?

Frustratingly, no. Monday the 13th of June; Friday the 1st of July; Tuesday the 12th of July. No pattern whatsoever. He shoved the newspapers aside in frustration, and took a ferocious bite out of his doughnut.

5

During the night, a long, deep crack had appeared in the village *pétanque* pitch. The Municipal Maintenance Department was looking into it.

Unfortunately, this being August, the Municipal Maintenance Department – not overmanned at the best of times – was reduced to a force of one; and he hadn't the faintest idea what to do about it. In the conversation around the village bar, there were muttered accusations of over-irrigation, lowering the water table and causing subsidence – but not a lot of practical propositions for dealing with the problem.

Even less fortunately, the disaster had occurred at the worst possible moment: in the week of the annual summer fête, and just two days before the most important competition of the year. Gloom and despondency fell upon the village, but Hugo gallantly came to the rescue.

'I said they could use our pitch,' he announced.

Zoe and Claude greeted the news with less enthusiasm than he had anticipated.

'Well, *I* think it's a wonderful idea,' said Moira, supportively. 'The whole village was absolutely devastated at the prospect of having to cancel the match. It's an integral part of the fête – one of the highlights of their year; they were thrilled to bits when Hugo offered the use of our pitch. They're very attached to their traditions, you know.'

'Not half as attached as they are to their money,' said Claude, drily (though this was a little rich, coming from an Auvergnat).

'I don't think there's all that much money involved,' protested Hugo. 'The top prize is only five hundred francs, and the third prize is a rabbit.'

'It's not the prize money they're interested in,' said Zoe. 'It's the side-bets. You can see thousands of francs changing hands at some of these competitions.'

'Well, I don't care,' said Moira. 'It'll be fun. The people in the village have organized food and wine and everything; all we have to do is provide the venue, and sit back and enjoy it. And they said they'd waive the entry fee if we want to put up a team.'

'Now, there's an offer we can't refuse,' said Hugo, sportingly.

Albuisson made a cursory scan of Andrieu's three newspapers, but he too could find nothing significant about them. His thoughts were on a different tack.

'This car crash,' he said; he had the file out again, spread across his desk. 'It makes me wonder. If you really want to get at someone, tampering with their brakes is a pretty haphazard way of going about it. How do you know where they're going to be when the brakes fail? If they happen to be driving slowly along a flat road, then they just shift into first and put the handbrake on, and there's no harm done. If someone fixed up Chavanac's car, how could he be sure it was going to be hurtling down a mountain road at the appropriate time?'

'In an area like this, I'd have thought it was a fairly safe bet,' said Andrieu.

'Not necessarily. In the nature of things, most of us spend

just as much time going *up* mountain roads as we do coming down. Another thing: how were they to know he'd be alone in the car? Or even that he'd be driving it himself? What if his wife had been using it? Or if he had his kids with him?'

'Well, I think I know the answer to that one. The car he was driving was a two-seater sports model – a very tasty motor, in fact,' said Andrieu, with just a suspicion of envy. 'It's not what you'd call a family car, and they're not what you'd call a one-car family. I doubt if he'd have used the sports car for ferrying the kids about. He probably only drove it when he was on his own – you can see from the *kilométrage*: barely five thousand on the clock in almost six months; he obviously didn't use it all the time. In any case, the kind of person who'd do something like this probably wouldn't care too much if someone else was in the car. You don't mess around with cars if you're bothered about innocent bystanders – think what might have happened to those schoolchildren.'

'True enough,' agreed Albuisson. 'But how would someone know where the car was going to be when the brakes failed? Unless, of course . . .'

'The lunch in St-Flour?'

'That's what I'm wondering. If someone knew Chavanac was going to be there, could they have got at his car while he was in the hotel, timing it so that the brakes would be likely to fail as he was driving home? If they did, then the chance of a serious crash would be fairly high. Coming from there to St-Geraud, the road starts off relatively flat, even uphill in places. But if the problem is to do with leaking fluid, and it's escaping gradually, then presumably the brakes won't fail immediately. And by the time they do, it's downhill all the way.'

'And, when you think about it,' said Andrieu, 'when else could the car have been got at? The brakes were okay three days earlier, when it was in Combelle's, and since then it hadn't been used; it was presumably sitting in Chavanac's garage at home – and there was no indication of a break-in.'

'You're right.' Albuisson tapped the file. 'And according to Chavanac's statement in here, he hadn't even been to his office that morning. He'd been doing some work at home, and he left there some time after ten thirty and drove straight to St-Flour.

So the only time that the car was unattended and accessible was while he was in the hotel.'

'You want me to check where the car was parked?' said Andrieu.

Albuisson considered. 'Yes, why not. And while you're doing that, I might have a word with Albert Brunet.'

'What's that?' said Moira.

'What?'

'I thought I heard something.'

'Probably those kids in the orchard again,' said Hugo, lazily adjusting his position on the sun-lounger and pulling his hat over his eyes.

'I think you should go and have a look, darling.'

'Oh, let them be. They're not doing any harm.'

'You just can't be bothered to get up.'

'That's true,' he admitted.

Moira stood up in a huff. 'Oh, I'll go myself,' she said.

Hugo sighed. Zoe took a sip from a glass of white wine, and watched a rank of little white clouds above the Luberon, linking up like a chorus line and then slowly turning into a giant *baguette*.

'World's most boring job,' said Hugo, from under his hat. 'Provençal weather forecaster. "Today will be hot and sunny. Tomorrow will be hot and sunny. And the long-range forecast: hot and sunny."'

Moira returned.

'Was it kids?' he said.

'It would appear so.'

'What did I tell you?'

'It does no harm to check. Oh, darling, stop that, it's not nice.'

'I wasn't doing anything.'

'Not you, Hugo. I'm talking to Chiara.'

Chiara, sitting happily by the poolside, picking her nose and sampling the proceeds, thought it was perfectly nice. But she did as she was told and toddled off in search of alternative amusements.

Fredy arrived, at a loose end. Lucie had gone riding with the Dutch contingent, Chiara was too young to be an interesting companion, and everyone else was too old. They just lay around all the time, and whenever he suggested doing anything, they groaned and complained it was too hot.

He flopped sulkily into a deckchair, and said loudly – and in English – 'I'm *bored*!'

'Language!' said Moira, sternly. 'A franc in the box, please.'

'Oh, sod off,' retorted Fredy.

'Fredy!' rebuked Zoe. 'How dare you be so rude!'

'Well, why do we have to do what she says? It's stupid, all these rules. Anyway, Dad says we've to practise our English.'

Claude, unwilling to be drawn into the argument, let out a gentle snore so that everyone would know he was asleep. Zoe reluctantly got up and grabbed Fredy by the ear, making him howl in several languages at once.

'Come on,' she said, relenting. 'I'll thrash you at table-tennis.'

'Boys!' muttered Moira, in exasperation, once they were out of earshot.

'It's just a phase he's going through,' said Hugo.

Albert Brunet, as he was never slow to remind you, had started life sixty-eight years ago in a one-roomed cottage with dirt floors. He had come a long way since then. Not in distance: the piss-poor hamlet where he first saw the light of day was no more than a few kilometres away (tourist coaches drove through it now, and guides pointed out the very cottage, with varying degrees of accuracy). But nowadays Brunet lived in some style, in a grand house approached through imposing gateposts topped with absurd stone lions, and a long straight driveway lined with lime trees.

Some nineteenth-century cattle baron, torn between practicality and pretension, had built this house four-square against the worst of the Auvergne weather, a solid pile of sombre, dark grey stone – and then dressed it up in preposterous fairytale towers and turrets, like a pig in a party frock. Albuisson parked at the end of the drive, and trekked up a monumental staircase that would not have disgraced Versailles. Brunet met him at the top with a hearty handshake.

'You're out of puff, old son. Ought to get yourself in shape.'

Albuisson outwardly smiled and inwardly cringed. Long ago, his father and Albert Brunet had been friends, and as a child he had been subjected to many a patronizing pat on the head from the great man, and a wealth of lectures on life and politics.

'How's your mother? Keeping well, I hope.'

Albuisson nodded non-committally. His mother had never liked Brunet. He followed the older man through a hallway and into a spacious, well-furnished room with tapestry-hung walls and graceful windows looking out on summer lawns.

'So what can I do for you?'

Albuisson explained.

'Chavanac?' Brunet pursed his lips. 'Yes. An interesting young man.'

'But not your kind of politician?' Albuisson suggested.

'My dear Georges, my kind of politician no longer exists. It's another world, today. They want a different kind of animal. I'm sure Claude Chavanac will serve them very well. What he believes in – whether he believes in anything – I wouldn't like to say. But he's clever, and cleverness counts more than conviction these days.'

'So you wouldn't stand in his way?'

Brunet laughed. 'I think you over-estimate my influence, old son. I'm not in government now, you know; just a retired old warhorse put out to grass. They might ask my opinion – might even take some notice of it, if it suits their purposes – but if they want Chavanac, I'm in no position to stop them.'

Well, maybe not through conventional channels, thought Albuisson.

'What about other people?' he said. 'What do they think of him?'

'He's like any other prospective politician: there's those that like him, those that detest him, and those that don't give a toss as long as he doesn't upset their particular applecart.'

Albuisson smiled: now we get to it, he thought. Chavanac was on record as a fierce critic of vested interests in local politics. He said: 'Are there any applecarts *especially* at risk of overbalancing, would you say?'

'You mean,' said Brunet, with a worldly smile, 'someone afraid that Chavanac's going to expose him with his snout in the trough? Oh, I don't think so. Most rookie politicians talk about rooting out the sins of their predecessors – especially the lawyers; they're a self-righteous lot. Doesn't mean they ever do anything about it, though. Once they get a foot on the ladder, they find they've got more important things to think about – like how to make room for their own snouts. In any case, I don't think there's anyone round here with cause to worry. We may not all be virgins, but that doesn't make us whores.'

He caught sight of Albuisson glancing around the room, taking note of the furnishings, expensive carpets, *objets d'art*. 'You're pointing your finger at me?' he said, and laughed again – a bluff, good-tempered, man-of-the-people laugh. 'Well, I'll admit, I've made a few *sous* in my time. I've not turned down opportunities that came my way. But it's all out in the open. I've no fear of exposure from Chavanac; there's nothing to expose.'

'An honest politician?'

'Near enough.'

Albuisson walked to the window. There was a peacock parading across the lawn. He said: 'What about rivals? Does Chavanac have any?'

'Professionally, yes, of course he does. Politically – no, not seriously. He's not a big enough threat to anybody, yet. Give it a couple of years . . .'

'So you don't think there'd be anyone at that lunch in St-Flour who'd have had a good reason for trying to get rid of him?'

Brunet placed an avuncular arm around his shoulder. 'Listen, Georges: what happened to Claude Chavanac was nothing more than an unfortunate accident. Let's just be thankful it wasn't worse, eh?'

He stood, waving, at the top of the staircase, as Albuisson walked to his car.

'Take care,' he called. 'And don't forget to give my regards to your mother.'

6

Peace had broken out by breakfast. A truce had been negotiated: French would be spoken at dinner; for the rest of the day, everyone could speak whatever language they pleased. As a consequence, the French were speaking English and the English speaking French, while Claude, from time to time, would throw in a spot of German or Italian, just to be perverse.

Chiara, bewildered, had retreated into silence. It was not that she had any problem with languages; small children soak up new words like a sponge, whatever their provenance. She knew that different people had different names for things; she was wearing what she and Mummy called a frock, but Daddy always called it a dress, and cousin Lucie called it a *robe*. Nothing good about that. Except that now Lucie was calling it a dress, and Mummy was calling it a *robe*, and Chiara wasn't sure what she was supposed to call it, so she thought it best to keep quiet until she found out what was going on.

She pushed some runny egg yolk round her plate with her finger, to make interesting patterns. Daddy told her to stop it and eat her breakfast properly. Then Lucie came running in, bawling.

'Good heavens, what on earth's the matter?' said Aunt Zoe.

Lucie just blubbed and mumbled, and tugged Aunt Zoe's arm to make her go outside, so Aunt Zoe got up and went with her, and Daddy went too. Chiara slipped down off her chair, wiped her eggy hands on her whatever it was she was wearing, and followed them.

They went to the swimming pool, and Lucie pointed into the water, and Daddy said: 'Oh dear.' Chiara, unseen, padded softly to the edge of the pool and peered in.

The little cat that came to drink was lying under the water. It was dead. She knew that, because sometimes in the mornings they found frogs at the bottom of the water like this, and Daddy said that's what they were: dead. He always fished them out with a net, and made the same joke every time, about eating their legs. But he never did – and he wouldn't let Fredy play with them, either; he just threw them away.

He didn't throw the cat away, though. Lucie was crying, and when Fredy came out and looked into the pool and said: 'Mmm. Barbecued kitty for dinner tonight, then?' she thumped him and said he was *horrid*, and she bet it was him that made the cat fall in the water and drowned it; and he got stroppy and whined that everybody blamed him for everything.

Aunt Zoe told them to stop fighting, and said it wasn't anyone's fault, it was just an accident. She said they all knew how the cat used to lean over the edge of the pool to drink the water, and it must have leaned too far and fallen in, and then it couldn't get out again.

Daddy said everyone had to go away and not look, and then he'd go into the pool and get the cat out. Fredy wanted to stay and watch, but Daddy promised him a clip round the ear if he didn't behave himself, so they all went back inside.

Lucie stopped crying and said there had to be a proper funeral, with a coffin and flowers and everything. Chiara didn't know what a coffin was, but it turned out to be a cardboard box from the supermarket. She helped Lucie pick some flowers, and Fredy said he didn't know what all the fuss was about, it was only a cat.

But anyway, Daddy dug a big hole under a tree in the orchard, and then they all went out and stood round it, and Lucie put the box with the cat in it into the hole. Aunt Zoe said a little poem in French, and then Daddy put the soil back over the box and filled in the hole, and Lucie and Chiara laid the flowers on top. So that's what a funeral is, Chiara thought.

And nobody went in the pool for the rest of the day.

'Chavanac's car', said Andrieu, 'was left in a public car-park in the middle of the town, from just after twelve until round about a quarter past three. I talked to the doormen at the hotel where the lunch was held. There's an underground garage, but that was full, so Chavanac gave the keys to the doorman on duty and asked him to park the car. He showed me the parking space where he left it.'

'He remembered the exact parking space, after all this time?' said Albuisson.

'He remembered the whole thing very well – partly because of the accident afterwards, partly because of the car itself. He said he'd always dreamt of owning a car like that. He admitted he took it right round the block, just so he could drive it for a few minutes. Said it was a beautiful motor, went like a dream – and there was nothing wrong with the brakes, as far as he could tell.'

'And this parking space: where was it?'

'Right out in the open. People walking past all the time. You couldn't mess about with a car there without being seen.'

Albuisson considered. 'But if anyone did see, would they have taken any notice? You see a car in a car-park, someone's got the bonnet up, or they've jacked it up and they're fiddling around underneath – you don't think anything of it, do you? You think there must be something wrong with the car, and it's just the owner trying to fix it.'

'Yes, but you'd notice a car like that. You don't see all that many of them around – well, maybe in Paris or down the Riviera, but not here. And, don't forget, the accident was in all the papers and on the TV news, with plenty of pictures of the car. If people had walked past and seen someone apparently working on it, and then later heard that a car of that kind had been involved in an unexplained accident, I'm sure at least one of them would have come forward and said something – even if they'd thought nothing of it at the time. With an ordinary car, you might get away with it – people might not make the connection – but with a car that stands out in a crowd, you'd be taking a hell of a risk of being identified.'

'I suppose so. What did the doorman do with the keys, after he'd parked the car?'

'He left them at the hotel reception desk, with a note saying where he'd put the car. He finished his shift about an hour later, so there was another guy on duty when Chavanac came to pick up the keys. The second guy says he offered to get the car and bring it round to the hotel – he wanted a chance to drive it, too – but Chavanac said no, he'd walk over and get it for himself.'

'So the question is,' said Albuisson, 'was the car in the car-park all that time? Or could it have been taken somewhere else in the meantime? Where exactly did the doorman put the keys? Were they locked away?'

'No; they were on a hook behind the desk. I don't think it would have been that easy for just anyone to get at them, though, even if they knew where to look. It would have had to be one of the staff.'

'I think a few more questions might be in order,' said Albuisson.

A good crowd had turned out for the *pétanque* match, visitors and locals alike. The Municipal Maintenance Department and his cousin Jean had arrived early to set up trestle tables and sunshades on the parched expanse of lawn beside the pitch, and then the fishmonger arrived with his refrigerated van and drove across the flowerbeds to park beneath a tree. Relays of village ladies ferried food and drink to the tables or the fish van, according to perishability. Enormous bowls of a formidable *aïoli* filled the summer air with the heady scent of garlic.

Claude, pleading injury, had absconded to a shady spot at the farthest corner of the orchard, in the company of a nicely chilled bottle of *rosé* and some light reading matter. But Hugo tracked him down, all the same.

'You'll have to come and help out,' he called across the orchard. 'We're a man short.'

Claude tapped his bad leg. 'Excused games,' he said.

'Nonsense!' cried Hugo, who had been at the *pastis* and was ready for anything. 'You don't have to move about. That's the whole point. You're supposed to stand still with your feet together.'

'Sorry,' said Claude. 'I don't play.'

'Don't be ridiculous! You're a Frenchman. All Frenchmen play *boules*.'

Claude judged that this was probably not the moment to attempt to explain the sociological status of the game, nor to elaborate upon the distinctions between *boules*, *pétanque* and *jeu provençal*, which might seem inconsequential to an Englishman but could trigger small wars among the French. And, besides, half a bottle of Provençal pink was making him feel almost sociable.

'Oh, all right,' he said.

The match was in full swing, with the mayor presiding over the scoreboard. Players lined up in teams of three, from the thoroughly frivolous to the deadly serious. Hugo had organized the household into male and female teams – Moira, Zoe and Lucie versus himself, Fredy and Claude – and they stood on the sidelines awaiting their turn to play.

A crack team from the village smugly dispatched the German entry. An apparently unpromising trio turned out to have a secret weapon in the form of Madame P, who took gleeful satisfaction in dislodging an opponent's certain winner with a well-placed and ferocious spoiler. The Dutch beat a party of Belgians, but were then seen off by a nun and two children. The Hippopotamus, clad in white, applauded at all the wrong moments, while the Newlyweds stood apart at the back of the crowd, and Hugo darted about taking photographs until it was time for his team to take the pitch.

They were pitted against strong local opposition.

'This is going to be so humiliating,' moaned Fredy, who hadn't wanted to play in the first place. 'Dad's utterly useless. He's never played in his life. We'd have been better off with Chiara.'

'Where is Chiara, incidentally?' said Moira.

'Come on, it's only a game,' said Hugo, cheerfully, pushing Fredy towards the pitch. 'It's not the winning that matters, it's the taking part.'

What a load of crap, thought Fredy and Claude, simultaneously.

Hugo put in a creditable performance, despite a bizarre style that owed more to cricket than *pétanque*. Fredy's first attempt was good, but his second pitch displaced Hugo's near-certain winner. Claude, playing last, manoeuvred himself awkwardly into position, narrowed his eyes, pitched low and went wide.

'What did I tell you?' said Fredy.

Claude shrugged. What the hell, he thought, and made his second pitch high. To his considerable surprise, the *boule* thudded to the ground a centimetre from the *cochonet*.

'Oo!' said the crowd.

'Beginner's luck,' said Claude, modestly. But next time round, he did it again. There was a flurry of activity at the back of the crowd, as the betting was adjusted.

'I never knew you could play like that,' said Fredy.

'Oh ye of little faith,' said Claude, thinking, neither did I.

Moira, searching for Chiara, came upon the Newlyweds emerging from the undergrowth beyond the poolhouse, looking dishevelled and slightly embarrassed.

'Hello,' she said.

The husband smiled goofily. He was just a boy, really; and no oil painting, tall and gangly with thin hair and thick glasses. He stammered, too. 'H-h-hot, isn't it?' he said. His forehead was pimply and beaded with sweat.

Well, he probably has a very nice nature, Moira thought charitably. She gestured at the pool. 'Have a swim, if you like. That'll cool you down.' Most of the visitors had villas with pools of their own, but she happened to know that these two were renting a little house in the village; she thought they might appreciate the offer.

But the girl snapped: 'No way,' and walked off.

Moira stared at her. The boy said, apologetically: 'She c-can't s-swim. She's afraid of the water. Her little s-s-sister d-drowned when she was a child. She was there; she s-s-saw it all.'

'Oh, I see,' said Moira, more sympathetically. 'But I'd have thought that gave her all the more reason to learn. Everyone should know how to swim.'

'I know, but she c-c-can't. It's ps-ps-psychological.'

'Oh, well,' said Moira, 'I suppose it's none of my business. You haven't seen a little girl anywhere, have you? In a blue dress?'

'Yes, she was over there just now, by that f-f-field of tomatoes.'

Chiara had discovered that overripe, squishy tomatoes lying on the ground would burst to gloriously messy effect when she jumped on them.

'God, look at the state of you!' said Moira – but gently, of course, because the experts agreed that it was quite wrong to shout at a child.

'Oh, there you are,' said Zoe, when they arrived back at the *pétanque* pitch. 'We're on next.'

'This should be good,' sniggered Fredy.

'Actually,' said Hugo, watching them play, 'Moira's not bad at this.'

But the opposition were better.

'An honourable defeat,' said Hugo.

'It could have been worse,' conceded Zoe. 'At least we weren't beaten by the nun and the two kids.'

Claude absent-mindedly licked an ice-cream that Lucie had considerately brought him. It tasted oddly of fish. She stood on tiptoe and whispered in his ear: 'That's the bimbo lady, over there.'

Joelle Rocard was wearing a halter top and a very small pair of shorts. Claude instinctively assessed her, as an art expert might assess a Titian. No: a Rubens. Definitely a Rubens. Then he became conscious of what he was doing, and told himself to stop it.

Philippe Rocard had spotted him. Claude saw him saying something to his wife; she looked in his direction, and then they were both coming towards him. He took a deep breath.

'Hello, there!' said Rocard. He was smiling. 'Claude Chavanac, isn't it? Remember me? I met your wife up in the village the other day.' He smiled at Lucie. 'Is this your little girl?'

So far, so good, thought Claude, with some relief.

On the pitch, proceedings had taken a serious turn. By now, most of the foreigners had been eliminated, and even the nun and the children had succumbed to a determined attack by a heavyweight team from Roussillon. But the locals weren't having it all their own way: the two young men from Suffolk, having co-opted the pensioner from Orléans to join their team, had come from nowhere to lay waste the opposition. The odds were in complete disarray, and the mayor was anxiously contemplating the humiliation of having to award the cup to strangers (and some are stranger than others, he thought).

The Hippopotamus sailed by, all in white, with her tiny companion in attendance. She glared at Hugo as she passed.

'What did you do to offend her?' asked Zoe.

'I just asked if she'd seen much of Captain Ahab recently.'

'I can't take you anywhere,' sighed Moira.

Joelle Rocard was saying to Claude: 'Philippe's been telling me all about you.'

God, I hope not, thought Claude.

Everything came out all right in the end. The outsiders were eliminated in the semi-final, and local honour was preserved.

'It's a fix,' complained Hugo. 'They could have won. The old man threw it.'

'He's no fool,' said Zoe.

So the postman, the barman and the electrician won the cup, as usual. The crowd decamped to the trestle tables, and afterwards they all smelt of garlic for days.

7

Albuisson paid a call on the hotel in St-Flour, taking the doormen quite by surprise. They had thought it was all over. The younger policeman had been amiable, and gone away apparently satisfied; they hadn't been expecting a return visit. Albuisson was not so amiable. He made them go through it, together and separately, over and over again.

Back in St-Geraud, he told Andrieu: 'There'something going on there. I'm not sure what it is, but there's definitely something going on.'

Moira had organized an expedition to the Fontaine de Vaucluse. The arrangements had been made over dinner the previous evening. Claude had opted out; most of the sights were acccessible only on foot, with an uneven, rocky path to the *fontaine* itself, and he wasn't quite up to that yet.

The rest of them piled into the Chavanacs' Citroën, with Zoe at the wheel because she knew the way. Fredy roared with approval every time she made the tyres squeal, while Hugo sat silently praying to St Christopher, and Moira, oblivious, sat in the back, reading aloud from the guidebook.

They found a car-park, paid their dues to a pompous little functionary, and walked the rest of the way into the town.

'There's a hell of a lot of people here,' remarked Hugo.

'"The most-visited natural site in the whole of France",' read Moira.

'This is nothing,' said Zoe. 'You should see it on a Sunday afternoon. It's like Oxford Circus in the rush hour.'

Inevitably, there was a dispute. Moira insisted they should all visit the Petrarch museum. Fredy dissented, vigorously.

'What's so great about some boring old poet who's been dead about a thousand years?'

'Only around six hundred, actually, Fredy,' said Moira, solemnly checking her dates. '"Petrarch: 1304 to 1374".'

'Big deal,' said Fredy, to whom anything more than ten minutes was a long time. He wanted to see the museum of torture and punishment, which boasted, amongst other attractions, a working guillotine.

'Don't tempt me,' said Zoe.

'Petrarch was a great lyric poet,' explained Moira. 'He lived in Avignon but he had a country house here for many years. He was passionately in love with a lady called Laura, but she was married to someone else.'

'Yuk,' said Fredy.

Hugo said, actually, he'd rather like a look at the Resistance museum. So they compromised: Moira to the Petrarch museum with Lucie, who thought it all sounded terribly romantic; Hugo and Fredy to the *Musée de la Résistance*.

Zoe stayed outside with Chiara. Not a fan of museums, she was quite content to sit at the riverside and let herself be mesmerised by the fast-flowing water, while Chiara sucked on something disgustingly sticky purchased from one of the tacky tourist stalls along the footpath.

Despite all the trappings of tourism – the bars and pizza stands and stalls selling hideous pottery and a hundred things to do with lavender, the ubiquitous North Africans with suitcases of belts and bangles laid out on the pavement, the coach parties all talking at the tops of their voices and none of them listening – despite all that, the place somehow managed to retain its dignity.

Great white cliffs soared dizzyingly up to a cobalt sky, and the river slid past endlessly, endlessly green: pale and almost fluorescent running shallow over limestone rocks, dark where it flowed deep, astonishingly vivid where it swirled through the underwater forest of weed.

Zoe took Chiara down a little path to the water's edge, let her take off her shoes and dangle her feet in the shallows. The current was fascinating in its complexity; here, almost still; further in, the surface was as smooth and innocent as glass, but the water beneath flowed fast and determined, flattening the long strands of weed. In places, it twisted and turned and eddied, and foamed against the rocks; in others, it bobbed as gently as bathwater.

Across the river, a floating raft of weed and broken branches, washed down on the current, had accumulated in a little sheltered harbour formed where the bank jutted out at an angle. As Zoe watched, a sleek brown creature emerged from the water and climbed upon the raft. Passing children stopped to look, calling their parents to come and see. A small crowd gathered – among them, Zoe noticed, the Newlyweds.

Someone said: 'What is it?', and someone else said: 'It's a little beaver.' 'No, it's not.' 'Well, what is it, then?' 'It's some kind of water-rat.' 'Ugh.' 'That's not a rat. It's nice; rats are horrid.'

'Look,' said Zoe to Chiara. 'See the animal, over there?'

Chiara stared, transfixed. A giant hamster! The animal stared back, bright black button eyes and two little yellow front teeth, its coat rich and glossy. Then, tired of all the attention, it dived off the raft again, and was lost in the deeper, darker waters.

Oh dear, sighed Chiara. Dead. That's what happened to animals in water: frogs, cats, giant hamsters. She pictured it, lying at the bottom of the river. She was not unduly distressed. Someone would probably give it a funeral.

On the terrace at the shady side of the villa, Claude reclined on a lounger, half-asleep. A fat volume of political memoirs lay open on his lap. Little whispers of breeze sashayed through the leaves of the vine that sprawled across the trellis overhead.

The sound of a car horn jolted him awake. It was insistent, designed to attract his attention. He manoeuvred his crutches into position, got to his feet and made his way through the house.

Outside, in the drive, stood the decrepit old van that belonged to Jean, cousin of the Municipal Maintenance Department. He had come to pick up the trestle tables left behind after the *pétanque* match, he said. Was that all right? Claude told him to go right ahead.

The tables had been folded and left in a pile at the edge of the pitch. They were large tables, and Jean was a very small fellow. He picked up the first one, and staggered with it towards the van.

Claude said: 'I'd give you a hand if I could, but . . .'

'Not to worry. The others'll be here in a minute.'

In due course, two more vans arrived, disgorging the plumber, the electrician, the Municipal Maintenance Department himself, and Madame P's nephew, Paul. Between them, they soon had the tables in the vans.

The electrician surveyed the empty pitch.

'Bit of a mess, isn't it?'

'That's okay,' said Claude. He was feeling very *laissez-faire* today.

'No, wouldn't want to leave it like that. Won't take a minute.'

They set about smoothing and grooming the sand with assorted brushes and rakes from the Municipal Maintenance van, then stood back to admire their handiwork.

'That's better,' said Jean.

'Looks nice, that,' said the electrician.

They all stood there, nodding appreciatively. Claude knew exactly what they were up to. The public *pétanque* pitch remained rent asunder, and the vertiginous arrangement of the village meant that there was nowhere else flat enough to provide even a poor substitute. They were a bunch of addicts in search of a fix.

'Go ahead and play, if you like,' he said.

They looked at him wide-eyed, as though the thought had never crossed their minds.

'Well,' said the plumber, slowly, 'as it happens, I do have my *boules* in the van.'

And, by a curious coincidence, so did all the rest of them.

'Problem is, there's an odd number of us,' said Jean. He turned to Claude. 'You don't fancy a game, do you?'

'Me?' said Claude.

'Why not? You were pretty nifty at the match the other day,' said Paul.

'I don't have any *boules*.'

'That's all right,' said the Municipal Maintenance Department. 'I've got a spare set in the van.'

The party reassembled, by prior agreement, at the paper mill. Fredy, though still complaining, had secretly rather enjoyed the Resistance museum. Lucie had been mildly bored by Petrarch, but she liked the paper mill: the big mossy water wheel, the huge wooden beams and rollers, the thick hand-made paper with flowers and leaves pressed into it. She was eager to take back a sheet of it, as a gift for the absent Claude. Zoe tried to persuade her that the plain ones were best, but she insisted upon buying one printed with a glutinous poem devoted to an improbably perfect Papa.

'Ah yes, that sounds just like your father,' said Zoe.

They came out into the sunshine, and walked with the crowd along the path to the eponymous *fontaine*.

'Wow!' said Hugo.

An immense cavern gaped at the foot of the towering cliff. Water gushed up from unseen depths and rolled away relentlessly.

'"The source of the River Sorgue",' read Moira. '"The water rises through a siphon effect from a great underground river."'

Hugo peered warily into the abyss.

'How deep is it?'

'Nobody knows,' said Fredy. He was clued up on this; on a previous visit, he and Claude had explored the speleological museum. 'They've sent down diving bells and mini-submarines,' he said. 'Even Jacques Cousteau's been down there, hundreds and hundreds of metres, but no one's ever got to the bottom.'

'Maybe there isn't one,' said Lucie, wide-eyed. 'Maybe it goes down and down forever.'

'Don't be stupid,' said Fredy, scathing as only a boy with a younger sister can be. 'That would mean it went right through the earth and out the other side, so all the water would come pouring out in Australia.'

'It's certainly impressive,' said Hugo, wondering incidentally how anyone had managed to get graffiti quite so far up the sheer wall on the far side of the cavern.

'It's quite tame at the moment,' said Zoe. 'It's even more impressive after heavy rain.'

'I can imagine.'

'Oh, look,' said Moira. 'Isn't that the Newlyweds?'

The two of them were standing a few metres away, close to the water. The boy was gazing at the girl, and the girl was gazing at the river.

'Yes, I saw them earlier,' said Zoe. 'They're a strange pair, aren't they? I wonder what she sees in him. He's not exactly God's gift.'

'Hidden depths, I expect,' said Moira. 'Or maybe it's the motor bike. I must say, I'm surprised to see them here. I was talking to them out by our swimming pool the other day – you know, the day of the *pétanque* match – and he said she's terrified of water. Apparently, she had a sister who drowned. But look at her now, staring into the river.'

'Some people are fascinated by the things they fear most.'

'I think Chiara's getting a wee bit tired,' said Hugo. 'Shall we go?'

Back at the villa, Claude was nowhere to be seen. Zoe found him on the terrace outside their bedroom, staring across the vineyards towards the Luberon, a glass of whisky on the table beside him.

'It's a bit early for the hard stuff, isn't it?' she said.

He looked at the whisky as though he'd never seen it before.

She said: 'What's the matter? What have you been up to?'

'Playing *pétanque* with a bunch of characters from the village.'

'You? Fraternising with the working classes? What on earth came over you?'

He scowled. 'You talk as though I'm Marie Antoinette.'

'Sometimes you behave like Marie Antoinette. Let's face it, Claude: you are not a man of the people.'

'As a matter of act, I had a bloody good time,' he said; and it was true. Until he began to play, he hadn't realized just how much, over the weeks of enforced inactivity, he'd been missing the buzz of competition. Once he was engrossed in the game, it didn't matter who the other players were; they were all on the same plane. And, contrary to all his expectations, he'd enjoyed their company, their scabrous banter and disrespectful wit.

'It was so good that it drove you to the bottle?' said Zoe.

'No, it wasn't that.' Claude hauled himself to his feet. 'I'll show you.'

Stepping out on the vine-covered terrace downstairs, she couldn't work out at first what he wanted her to see. The lounger, with its brightly patterned cushions, stood where it always stood. Claude's book lay on the ground beside it. Then she saw the rock.

It was a solid lump of limestone, roughly dressed, about half a metre square and not quite so thick. It lay on the ground at the back of the lounger, in a mess of vine leaves and splintered wood. She looked up.

There was a gash in the trellis, and through it she could see the roof, and the gap in the row of rocks along the edge-tiles, like a missing tooth. The rock had fallen from the roof, crashed through the trellis, and smashed into the head-rest of the lounger with sufficient force to snap it off at the hinges.

'Jesus!' she said. 'When did this happen?'

'I don't know exactly. It was while I was playing *pétanque* with the blokes from the village. If they hadn't turned up, that thing would have landed right on my head.'

Moira burst upon the scene, crying: 'Oh, there you are. I've . . .'

She stopped, taking in the situation.

'You see: I told you those rocks were bloody dangerous,' she said.

8

'I hear you've been visiting Albert Brunet,' said the voice on the telephone.

'Who told you that, Mother?' said Albuisson.

'Denise.'

Denise Brunet: the old rogue's wife. What was she up to, talking to his mother? True, they knew each other from way back, but they were never bosom friends and he wasn't aware they'd kept in touch.

'She called by the other day,' his mother said, 'with some photographs – old ones; she'd been sorting through some things in an old trunk, and she'd found a box full of them. There were some of your father; she thought I might like to have them. Nice of her, wasn't it? There's one or two very good ones; I thought I might have them framed. You can take a look at them some time, if you come round; see what you think.'

He visited assiduously, once a week, and yet she talked as though he never came. What she really wanted was all of them there round the table, every Sunday – Georges, his sisters, and all their families, cousins and aunts and uncles, just like the old days. But it wasn't like the old days. People lived their lives differently now.

'Did she have any news?' he said.

'Who?' Advancing age had given her the attention span of a goldfish.

'Denise Brunet.'

'Oh, she was just saying what a relief it was to be back home for good. She says Paris is getting worse – the crowds, traffic, noise, crime, immigrants, you wouldn't believe it; she was glad to get out. I'm not surprised. Cities are for young people. She said Albert was saying how nice it was to see you again after all this time, and how well you'd done to get so high up the ranks.'

Now, what was that supposed to mean?

Albuisson was a realist; he knew his limitations. He'd done well enough, but not as well as he would have liked. He was methodical, disciplined, stuck to the rules; and if he'd never had that spark of genius – or luck – that catapulted others to glory, he also lacked the recklessness and hubris that could bring them just as quickly crashing down.

He'd always felt he deserved more credit than he got, but he'd learned that it was counter-productive to complain. So he had simply got on with the job and adjusted his expectations. When he started, his sights had been set on the top of the ladder, but now he was merely concerned to consolidate what modest gains he had achieved.

There had been a spell of treading water, with dull jobs and sideways promotions; but last year's Littleton murder case, with all the attendant publicity, had given his career new momentum. He reckoned that now, so long as he turned in a competent performance and avoided making waves, that momentum was enough to carry him steadily forward – not on the fast track, admittedly, but he was prepared to settle for a branch line.

He could define that as success on his own terms; but it hardly merited fulsome compliments. Perhaps Brunet was being ironic. Or just tactful.

He asked his mother: 'Did Denise say anything else?'

'Well, she mentioned that they were surprised at you investigating this Chavanac business. She was asking if some new evidence had come up, and had somebody given you the go-ahead to reopen the enquiry? Of course, I said I knew nothing about it. He never tells me anything, I said. She says her two are just the same. You remember them? Albertine and Denis. I always thought that was unusual, calling the girl after the father and the boy after the mother. Albertine's got six children now – imagine, six! And he's doing very well for himself. Property, I think she said.'

'Good for him.' said Albuisson, pondering. 'Listen, I must go. I've got work to do.'

His mother sighed. 'Oh, well,' she said. 'I suppose I'll be seeing you, some time.'

The caretaker's name was Louis Godard, but he was known for some unexplained reason as Gigi. His head went up and down like an oil derrick: up to the roof, down to the rock on the ground.

'Well, I don't know,' he said. 'First time I've seen anything like this.'

He bent down to test the weight of the rock. It was heavy.

'It must have been unbalanced,' said Moira. 'Not lying flat, or too close to the edge, or something.'

Gigi said: 'If it was, it's been like that for months. I checked the place over at the end of the winter; there's been nobody up there since. We had some torrential rain in the spring, and some almighty *mistrals* – why didn't it come down then? Why now, on a hot summer's day, when there's hardly a breath of wind?'

He put a ladder against the wall, shinned up it and scrambled on to the roof. He was a tubby, bow-legged little man, not at first sight a natural athlete, but he moved with agile confidence on the shallow-pitched roof. He pushed and tugged at some of the other rocks balanced along the edge.

'See?' he said. 'They're not easy to shift, these things.'

'Can you see anything else up there?' said Hugo.

'Well, there's a couple of loose tiles, and it looks like there's a bird's nest under the eaves there. But I can't see how that's going to dislodge a dirty great rock.'

'I reckon it was the giant hamster,' said Fredy, mischievously.

'The what?' said Gigi.

Hugo said: 'Some of us have heard noises in the roof at night. We thought some kind of animal must have got in there.'

'Well, we can soon see about that.'

Gigi scuttled down the ladder and waddled off around the corner, with Hugo and Fredy in pursuit.

'You can get into the roof-space from the garage,' he said.

The garage was like a cave, with rough stone walls. Old boxes and crates and dismembered bits of furniture lay about the perimeter.

'Of course, it wouldn't have been a garage in the old days,' said Gigi. 'It was some kind of store-room. And the roof-space up above would have been used for storage as well.'

He hauled out a crate, stood on it and reached up to pull down a trapdoor in the roof. A rickety ladder descended with it. He climbed up followed by Fredy, eagerly, and Hugo, warily.

'Careful where you walk,' said Gigi. 'Stay on the main joists if you can.'

In the roof-space it was dark and hot as an oven. Spears of dusty light slid through here and there, where tiles were askew. Gigi had a torch; he switched it on and swung the beam around the floor, illuminating cobwebs and emptiness.

Fredy saw something and went to look.

'What is it?' asked Hugo.

'Just some empty pistachio shells,' said Fredy, disappointed.

'I expect you must have dropped them,' Hugo said to Gigi.

'Not me. I don't eat nuts of any kind. I'm allergic to them.'

'Where did they come from, then?'

'Dunno. There was a couple of blokes up here last autumn, fixing a bit of wiring. They probably dropped them.' Gigi shone the beam into dark corners. 'A few mouse droppings,' he said. 'But that's all. Certainly no sign of giant hamsters.'

Hugo said: 'Well, it was just a thought.'

Andrieu went back to the hotel. Now the doormen were getting really rattled; but he wasn't certain if that was just the natural nervousness of innocent punters inexplicably hounded by persistent police – on a Saturday, even – or if it was something more sinister.

He turned his attention to the other hotel staff. There were two receptionists; the first had been on duty in the morning, the second in the afternoon, and they had overlapped for the busier lunchtime period. The first was a perky young woman, confident in her recollections. She remembered Claude Chavanac arriving and handing his car keys to the doorman, Gilbert; she'd seen Gilbert go out with the keys in his hand, and come back about five minutes later.

'You're sure it was only five minutes?'

'Could have been ten, I suppose, but it certainly wasn't any more than that.'

'Did you see what he did with the car keys when he came back?'

'He put them on a hook, down here behind the reception desk.'

'Could anyone have taken them off the hook?'

'I doubt it. I'm sure I'd have seen them if they did.'

The second receptionist was older, with a wedding ring and a harassed expression. She had been on duty when Chavanac left the hotel. Henri, the afternoon-shift doorman, had come over and asked her to pass him the keys from the hook behind the desk.

'Had they been there all the time you were on duty?' Andrieu said.

'I don't know; I suppose so. I can't say I noticed them – but why should I? Nobody said anything to me about them being there. The first I knew of it was when Henri asked me to hand them over.'

So there we have it, thought Andrieu. The two doormen and the younger receptionist adamant that the car keys had been safely stowed away behind the desk all the time; the older receptionist vaguer, but with nothing to say to cast doubt on their version of events. So why had Albuisson thought they were lying? And why was he inclined to agree?

'My, you are a little ray of sunshine today,' said Moira. 'What's the matter?'

'Oh, I don't know,' said Zoe.

They had walked to the village, leaving the men in charge of the children and domestic arrangements. Now they were sitting at a table outside the bar, with a pitcher of cold wine, watching the comings and goings in the square. Zoe was beginning to feel very slightly drunk on sun and wine, but instead of cheering her up it was making her morose.

'I suppose', she said, after some deliberation, 'that business with the rock was a bit unsettling. You start wondering if fate's got it in for you. And then there's Fredy. He used to be such a nice little boy; now he's turning into a monster.'

'It's just attention-seeking,' said Moira, who had read about these things.

'He gets lots of attention.'

'From you, perhaps. But what about Claude? What with his career, and this political business, and, um, whatever, I don't suppose he gets to spend much time with Fredy, does he? Fathers are very important, you know. Hugo has a schedule for spending quality time with Chiara, and I make sure he sticks to it.'

Zoe sighed. Moira put her in mind of the Roundheads, who were Right but Repulsive. She and Claude were rather more cavalier; no wonder Fredy was obnoxious.

'I even found myself wondering about the cat in the swimming pool,' she confessed. 'Did it fall or was it pushed?'

'You think Fredy might have done it?'

'It's not so much that I think he might have done it. It's just that I can't convince myself that the idea is out of the question.'

Moira took a swig of wine. 'After we'd buried that cat,' she said, 'I thought I'd use it as an opportunity to talk to Chiara about death and funerals and so forth. They say you mustn't shield children from death; you should introduce the subject as early as possible – but do it casually, not make a big thing of it. Then they won't see it as something strange and fearful, just as a natural event.

'I was going to do it when my father died, a couple of months ago, but I chickened out. I heard myself spouting all the usual euphemisms: Grandpa's gone to a nice place, Jesus will take good care of him – as if he'd gone on holiday to a hotel with particularly high standards of room service. I've regretted it ever since. So when we had the business with the cat, I thought, well, here's another chance; see if I can do it right this time. Start with the cat, and then lead on to Grandpa.'

'Did it work?'

'I'm not sure. She seemed rather confused.'

'Perhaps she's still a little too young.'

In fact, Chiara, being below the age of sentimentality, readily encompassed the concept of death and its associated rituals. She was just puzzled about the practicalities: how did they squeeze Grandpa into a cardboard box from the supermarket?

'I just hope she hasn't got the wrong message,' said Moira. 'You hear of people whose whole lives are ruined by childhood traumas – and so often they turn out to have arisen from quite trivial misunderstandings that nobody was even aware of at the time. God, sometimes I feel so inadequate.'

'You are inadequate,' said Zoe, bluntly. 'So am I. All parents are inadequate. The dice are loaded against us. Whatever good we do gets wiped out by other influences – their schools, their friends, TV, video games. But any harm we do seems to be indelible and screws them up for life.'

She lifted the wine pitcher and found it to be empty.

'Shall we have another one of these?'

'Should we?' said Moira.

'Why not? It's our day off, and we're not driving.'

'Oh, what the hell,' said Moira, recklessly.

*

Andrieu was surprised to find Albuisson at his desk on a Saturday morning.

'It's that second receptionist,' he told him. 'I'm sure she's the key.' He'd been thinking it over on the way back from St-Flour. 'The others are so certain,' he said. 'They're absolutely positive. They remember everything exactly, even though it was months ago – whereas, if what they're saying is true, it was hardly remarkable enough to stick in their minds at the time. And they all agree with each other. But the second receptionist is vague. I think one of the others is up to something – probably the doorman who took the keys in the first place. I don't think he did put them behind the desk; I think he gave them to somebody else, who then went out and did something to the car.

'But he's somehow persuaded the others to back up his story. The second woman won't go along with it, though – at least, not all the way. She won't contradict the story, but she won't support it either. She just says she doesn't know anything. But she's not happy about it, you can see that; she's uptight. I think, if we keep chipping away at her, she'll crack.'

'Forget it,' growled Albuisson.

'What?'

'I said forget it. Investigation over. Case closed.'

'Why?' Andrieu was shocked. 'We were just getting somewhere.'

'Orders,' said Albuisson. 'From on high.'

'How high?'

'Parrilaud.'

That high? Andrieu whistled softly.

'But isn't he on holiday?'

'Yes,' said Albuisson, crisply. 'Antibes.'

'Then how did he know about it?'

'Obviously, someone told him.'

'Yes, and I can imagine who,' said Andrieu, darkly.

'You imagine nothing,' said Albuisson. 'Do you understand? I don't want to hear any allegations, accusations, anything. The case is closed.'

Andrieu stared at him incredulously.

'But it's obvious what's happened! Parrilaud's been got at by

Brunet. Who else could it be? Who else is there who knows about the investigation, who's got a reason for wanting it stopped – and has enough clout to shift Parrilaud's fat arse off his sun lounger?' It was well known that Parrilaud, while displaying little respect for his officers' leisure time, took a dim view of police business intruding upon his own. 'I'll bet he was pleased,' said Andrieu.

'Oh, he was delighted,' said Albuisson, drily. 'I could tell by the tone of his voice.'

'He telephoned in person? From Antibes?'

Albuisson nodded.

'What did he say?'

'He said that unless I had any new evidence, there was no justification for reopening the case, and that if he found out I'd been wasting any more police time on it, or harassing innocent citizens, there'd be trouble. Or words to that effect.'

'That's ludicrous. How are we supposed to find new evidence if we're not allowed to investigate? And anyway, we do have evidence.'

'No, we don't. We just have supposition.'

'What about . . .' Andrieu racked his brains. 'What about that cigarette lighter you found in Chavanac's garden?'

Albuisson shrugged. 'I sent it to forensics, but of course they're short-handed at the moment, so it hasn't come back yet. But it's probably irrelevant anyway.'

'So you're suggesting we just drop the whole thing?'

'It's not a suggestion; it's a statement of fact. We have no option.'

'But that's crazy! We can't give up now. The very fact that Brunet's trying to get us off the case just goes to prove that we were getting too close for comfort.'

But Albuisson's face was a fixed, determined mask. 'We're not acting as individuals here,' he said. 'We're police officers. We do what we're told. There are rules, and we abide by them, whether we like it or not. And when I say "we",' he added, looking pointedly at Andrieu, 'I mean "we".'

'Yes, sir,' said Andrieu, sulkily. If there had been a cat within reach, he would have kicked it.

He spotted the three copies of *La Montagne* still lying at the side of Albuisson's desk.

'What about these?' he said.

Albuisson looked at them despondently.

'You'd better take them back to Chavanac's office,' he said.

9

'Another one of these, ladies?' The barman picked up the wine pitcher with a conspiratorial smile. 'Certainly.'

'He obviously thinks we're a pair of shameless hussies out on the razzle,' muttered Moira.

'He's not far wrong,' said Zoe. She was feeling a little more cheerful now. 'I'd watch out, if I were you. I think he fancies you.'

Moira tried not to feel flattered, as this would be politically incorrect. 'It won't last,' she said. 'Wait till he sees this.'

Joelle Rocard was coming down the main street, with a springy walk that made all the interesting bits of her bounce. She was heading towards the bar.

'I can't compete with that,' said Moira.

Joelle had spotted them.

'Hello, there,' she said. 'Can I join you?'

She pulled up a chair and sat down. The barman, returning, squinted down the front of her frock as he placed the refilled pitcher on the table.

'What did I tell you?' Moira murmured.

Zoe asked him to bring another glass for Joelle.

'Oh, that's very kind of you,' she said. 'I hope you don't mind me butting in. I feel a bit uncomfortable, coming here on my own. They're still quite old-fashioned in some of these little villages, aren't they? I mean, you don't often see a local woman going in a bar alone. Cheers!' She raised her glass and took a hearty gulp. 'There's something wrong with our car; Philippe knows how to fix it, but he needs some spare parts, so he's gone to Apt to see if he can get them. I hope he can; it's a special engine, and garages don't always have the bits in stock. If he can't, we'll be a bit stuck without transport. It's very nice here, but you want to go out sometimes, don't you? I mean, you must admit, there's not a lot of night-life. Still, Philippe's enjoying it, that's what matters. Course, he's been before; he used to come here with her ladyship – sorry; I shouldn't be rude. She was a friend of yours, wasn't she – his first wife, I mean.'

'We were neighbours,' Zoe said, 'but I wouldn't exactly say that we were friends. We were both out at work all day, so we didn't see much of each other.'

'Oh, well, that's all right then,' said Joelle. 'I never met her, myself. I've seen pictures of her, though, and I've heard people talk about her. She wasn't at all like me, was she? Very BCBG – and a bit of a Marie-Chantal, by the sound of it.'

'Excuse me,' said Moira to Zoe. 'What's she talking about?'

'BCBG is "*bon chic, bon genre*",' Zoe said. 'It means something like a Sloane Ranger. And a Marie-Chantal is a toffee-nosed snob.'

'Was this woman really like that?'

Zoe thought back. 'Yes, I suppose she was, rather.'

Joelle rambled on: 'Philippe's always loved this part of Provence,' she said. 'But after she'd gone, he stayed away – too many memories, I suppose; and I think he was afraid she might still be coming here, and they'd meet by accident. But this year he finally said he wanted to give it a try. Exorcise the ghost, he said.'

'So his first wife is dead, is she?' said Moira.

'No, she's in Bordeaux.'

'Oh, I see.'

'They split up years ago. His friends say he worshipped the ground she walked on. But then he found out she'd been sleeping around. They had a big bust-up about it, and that was the end of that. Till he met me, of course.'

She grinned, knowingly. Zoe refilled the glasses.

Andrieu stormed along the corridor towards Chavanac's office. He hated being pulled off a case just as he was getting his teeth into it – especially in circumstances like these. It *had* to be Brunet who had got to Parrilaud; there was no one else it could have been. And the very fact that he'd done it was as good as a confession of guilt.

As for Albuisson, that lily-livered tub of lard – all he cared about was protecting his pension. Follow the rules, go by the book; yes sir, no sir, three bags full sir; don't step out of line. Where was his sense of outrage? Where was his sense of justice?

Seething, he swept into Chavanac's office.

'Don't bother to knock, will you?'

The secretary was sitting there, still sorting papers.

'I didn't expect to see you here on a Saturday,' he said.

'You should see how much there is to do.' She scowled at him. 'What do you want this time?'

He flourished the newspapers.

'Just bringing these back.'

'Weren't they any good to you, then?'

'I wouldn't know. I've been kicked off the case.'

'Oh?' She showed a faint glimmer of interest. 'Given it to someone else, have they?'

'No. The powers that be have decided there's nothing to investigate. Waste of police time.'

He was tempted to unload the whole story, rant and rave and get it off his chest; but he didn't know her well enough to be sure that she'd keep it to herself. And if it got back to Albuisson that he'd told her, there was bound to be trouble.

'Well,' she said, 'I did wonder. I mean, they looked into it at the time, and they seemed pretty sure it was an accident.'

'Oh, yes?' The hell with discretion; he couldn't let that go unchallenged. 'And what about the other things – the fire, the break-in? They were just accidents too, were they?'

'I don't see why not. These things happen.'

'Just like that? One after the other? Doesn't that seem just a bit too much of a coincidence?'

She stuffed papers into a folder and shrugged. 'They always say these things come in threes.'

In threes, muttered Andrieu, scornfully, as he stomped back down the corridor. Like musketeers; colours on a flag; Huey, Dewey and Louie. Like . . .

Like newspapers, he thought.

*

Another flagon of wine had arrived. Joelle was getting misty-eyed. She watched the pensioner couple from Orléans, walking arm-in-arm up to the *alimentation*.

'Aren't they sweet?' she said. 'They've been married more than fifty years. Imagine! I wonder if we'll be like that, one day, me and Philippe. He's over eighty, you know.'

'Who is?'

'That old man. He was in hospital for two months earlier in the summer – heart bypass, pacemaker, all that stuff. She was telling me about it, round at your place, the day we had that *pétanque* match. You wouldn't know, to look at him, would you? Do you fancy some more of these pistachios?'

'Oh, not you again,' the girl said, as Andrieu came thundering back into the office. 'What is it now?'

'Those newspapers.' He scanned the room. 'What have you done with them?'

'I thought you said you were off the case.'

'Never mind that. Where are they?'

'They're over there.'

She had put them on top of a bookshelf. He picked them up, and looked around the room for a calendar. There was a large one pinned to the wall, alongside the door to Chavanac's office. He stood in front of it, counting.

'What are you doing?' she said.

'Do you remember the date of your boss's car accident?'

'It was a Thursday.' She narrowed her eyes, thinking. 'Thursday the 9th of June?'

'That's right. And the earliest of these newspapers is dated Monday the 13th of June. Now, what about the fire?'

'I don't remember exactly. Let's think: he was in hospital for about two weeks after the accident, and then he kicked up a fuss and they let him go home. The fire was just a few days after that. So it must have been near the end of the month.'

'Tuesday the 28th, to be precise. And the second of these newspapers is dated three days after that – Friday the 1st of July.'

She was getting the hang of it now.

'The break-in,' she said. 'There'll be a note of that in my diary. I had to find a locksmith who could go round and fit a new lock on the door of the apartment.' She flicked through the diary on her desk. 'Yes, here it is: July; Friday the 8th. What's the date on the third newspaper?'

'Tuesday the 12th of July.'

Outside the bar, things were getting rather giggly by now. The Newlyweds' motor bike roared into the square; they dismounted and walked to the bar, ordered beer and lit cigarettes.

'Have you noticed, people don't smoke like they used to,' said Moira. 'You used to go in a French café, and the air would be thick with Gauloises. Now, people either don't smoke at all, or they smoke American cigarettes like everybody else. It's not the same.'

'I thought you disapproved of smoking,' said Zoe.

'Well, yes, but you know what I mean.'

'Non-smokers are better in bed,' said Joelle, with the assurance of one who would be in a position to know. She squinted at the male Newlywed, and murmured, *sotto voce*: 'I don't reckon he's up to much. I bet those two won't be together in fifty years' time.'

'Why not?'

'Dunno, really. Just a feeling. They always look so . . . intense.'

'Aren't young lovers supposed to be intense?'

'Not like that,' said Joelle. 'You never see them laughing, do you? I mean, you've got to laugh sometimes; life's so bloody ridiculous.' She yawned. 'I feel ever so sleepy; it must be the wine. I think I'll go back to the house and have a lie-down.'

'Yes, I'm feeling a bit tired, too,' agreed Moira.

'And me,' said Zoe. 'Tired as a newt. I think it's time we went home.'

'That's the connection,' Andrieu said. 'Three events; three newspapers. The first issue's dated four days after the car crash. The second one is three days after the fire, and the third is four days after the break-in. Are you going to tell me that's a coincidence?'

'That's all very well,' said Chavanac's secretary, 'but what does it mean? I can see the significance of the dates, but what's the significance of the newspapers?'

'There,' said Andrieu, 'you have me. You say Chavanac looked through these papers, and couldn't find anything connected with himself?'

'That's right, and neither could I.'

'Maybe it's worth another look.'

He put the newspapers down on the table where she was working, shoved her filing aside, and pulled up a chair.

'What do you think you're doing?' she said.

'Two heads are better than one. I'll start at the beginning, you start at the end, and let's see if we can find something interesting.'

She hesitated, glancing at her pile of unfinished work.

'Oh, come on,' he said. 'Where's your spirit of adventure? You know you're as curious about this as I am.'

Which was true.

After a while, though, she said: 'Oh, this is hopeless. It's like when you're clearing out a cupboard, and you suddenly realize you've spent two hours reading all the old newspapers lining the shelves, and you've done nothing useful at all. I keep getting distracted by the stories, and forgetting what I'm meant to be looking for. And these advertisements: they make you wonder what sort of people are out there, don't they? Some of the things you see offered for sale – and as for the lonely hearts ads, well . . .'

Andrieu was staring at her.

'What's the matter with you?'

'Ads,' he said. 'I never thought of the ads. I had it in my head that it must be something in the news pages. I've been through these papers over and over again, and it never occurred to me to read the ads. What a pillock!'

He flicked to the advertisement section of the first issue. There were hundreds of little ads: jobs offered and wanted; homes for sale; cars for sale; legal announcements; restaurants, night-clubs; births, marriages and deaths. Like looking for a needle in a haystack.

There were people selling second-hand furniture, baby clothes, horse manure, pedigree kittens; someone had mislaid a

St Bernard dog (how, for heaven's sake?); someone was offering lessons in Mandarin Chinese.

He heard a sharp intake of breath, and looked up.

'Look in the Personal section,' the girl said.

He did. There were three items.

One said: 'Booboo: Love you always. Kissy.'

One said: 'G. Please don't sulk. Come home. T.'

And the third said: 'C.C.: Here's to the next time.'

10

Albuisson studied the three photocopies that Andrieu had placed in front of him. Each showed part of a column of newspaper small ads, enlarged, with one ad circled boldly in red, and two dates scrawled at the top. The ads all followed the same format; they were short and to the point. They read, in chronological order:

'C.C.: Here's to the next time.'

'C.C.: Don't you love the smell of pine?'

'C.C.: You can never replace the irreplaceable.'

'These dates are when the newspapers were published,' Andrieu said, pointing, 'and these are the dates when something happened – the car crash, the fire, the break-in. I think we can guess who C.C. is.'

Albuisson said nothing.

Impatient, Andrieu insisted: 'Parrilaud didn't tell you to lay off, full stop, did he? He said *if there was no new evidence*.'

Albuisson continued to peruse the photocopies.

'Well,' demanded Andrieu, 'is this new evidence, or what?'

'I wouldn't exactly call it *evidence* . . .' Albuisson said, slowly.

'Oh, for Christ's sake!'

'. . . but I might call it reasonable grounds for suspicion.'

Interpreting that as a definite maybe, and not waiting around to hear otherwise, Andrieu got on to the advertising department of *La Montagne*. They were happy to co-operate, but doubtful that they could be of much assistance. So many advertisements every day; who would remember? Some of the personal ads stuck in the mind, if they were really bizarre, but on the face of it there was nothing particularly striking about these. And in any case, whoever had dealt with the ads was probably on holiday by now; most people were. They had a lot of temporary staff in at the moment, students mostly.

Ah, yes, the payment; they might be able to trace that, if it had been made by cheque or credit card, or on account – though it was mainly the commercial advertisers with accounts, of course, not the personals. They'd look into it and call him back.

But when they did, the news was not encouraging. The three advertisements had been placed at different offices: the first in Clermont-Ferrand, the second in St-Geraud and the third in Mauriac. As far as could be seen from the records, they had all been paid in cash.

No one at Clermont or Mauriac had any recollection of how the advertisement had arrived; it could have been by phone, fax, mail or personal caller. No, they didn't keep original letters or faxes for more than a few days, in case of queries or complaints; if they'd kept every piece of paper that came into their offices, they wouldn't have room to move.

There was one spark of light: a man at the St-Geraud office who vaguely remembered coming in one morning before the mail arrived, and finding a hand-delivered envelope behind the door. It had contained a sheet of paper with copy for a lineage ad, together with the cash to pay for it. It might have been the 'C.C.' ad; it would have been about that time. But then again, it might not. He hadn't read it, just looked to find out what it was, and when he'd seen it was an ad, he'd passed it on to the copytaker.

He had seen the sheet of paper, though? Yes: as far as he could remember, it was typed. Well, not handwritten anyway. He couldn't say if it was typed, exactly, or if it came out of one of those computer printers; nobody uses typewriters any more, do they?

No, more's the pity, thought Andrieu. It must have been handy when forensics could pin down the very machine that produced a piece of typescript, by the little idiosyncrasies of the type bars and the letter forms. You can't do that with a laser printer.

And the envelope? As far as the man remembered, it was blank. Hadn't he thought that was odd? Well, no, he said; not if it was hand-delivered. If you were taking it yourself, you'd know where you wanted it to go, wouldn't you?

There was no denying the logic in that.

It was an excellent supper, but Albuisson wasn't enjoying it. His wife looked on with concern. It wasn't like Georges to toy with his food.

'You've barely touched your *terrine*,' she said. 'And you must try these tomatoes. It's a new variety; they have the most intense flavour.'

'Yes, dear.'

He dragged his attention back to the food, but it kept roaming off again when he wasn't looking. What was he to do about this Chavanac affair? The easy answer was in the rule book: go through all the formal procedures, make it an official investigation. But he knew damn well what would happen if he did that. Obstacles would mysteriously arise in his path.

All right, so, in the face of those newspaper ads, even Parillaud might be hard put to smother the case. But if Brunet – and Andrieu was right; it could only be Brunet – was really determined to keep him at bay, then the old fox had enough influence, in even higher places, to slow the whole thing down to an interminable crawl. Everyone would lose interest, while the evidence, if there was any, quietly faded away.

Well, so what? If his suspicions were unfounded, it wouldn't matter. It would be frustrating, but worse things happen. But suppose Brunet really was trying to harm – or even kill – Claude Chavanac? And suppose he tried again, and succeeded? How would he feel about that?

Of course, it wouldn't be his responsibility. That's the advantage of following the rules. If something goes amiss, but you've done everything by the book, then you can't be blamed.

But you can blame yourself.

In the wider scheme of things, he didn't feel that Chavanac's death would be a great blow to humanity. But the man was entitled to live his life. And he had a wife and children, a mother and father, probably brothers and sisters, too; Albuisson couldn't remember. What would he say to them, if something happened? I was only following orders?

They'd probably heard that one before.

Then what was the alternative? Ignore the newspaper ads and do nothing? Same problem. And even if he washed his hands of the affair, he couldn't guarantee that Andrieu would do the same. The boy had the bit between his teeth now; he was probably out there already, poking his nose into someone's business. It was his own fault; he should never have let him loose on this enquiry in the first place. But he couldn't turn back the clock.

Which left just one, uncomfortable option: continue the investigation, unsanctioned, in the hope of finding some incontrovertible evidence, which would then allow him to make it official without any fear of obstruction.

It went against all his instincts. It was unprofessional. And risky. He'd already been warned off once, and he couldn't afford to make an enemy as high up the ranks as Parrilaud. But did he, in all conscience, have any alternative?

The key question was, did he really believe that Chavanac was in danger?

Then he thought: Wait a minute. There is one factor in this equation that I haven't taken into account.

Claude Chavanac.

Didn't he have a right to know what was going on? If there was even the faintest suspicion that he might be in danger, shouldn't he be told? And, if he felt an enquiry was justified, then let him make it happen; he too had friends in high places.

All right, so that was just a fancy rationalization for what Andrieu would probably refer to as passing the buck. But from here it looked like the only solution.

Because Albuisson was keeping an eye on their house, Zoe Chavanac had given him the telephone number for their villa in Provence, in case he should need to contact them in an emergency. He could simply phone, tell Chavanac what had happened, let him decide what should be done.

No, he couldn't do that. It wasn't the kind of thing you could say over the telephone, just out of the blue: 'Enjoying your holiday? Oh, by the way, I think someone's trying to kill you; what do you want to do about it?'

It would be better done in person, face to face. How long would it take to drive down to that part of Provence? Not too long, if he used the motorway. There and back in one day might be a strain, in the heat, but with an overnight stay . . . He wouldn't have to tell anyone what he was doing; tomorrow, the 15th, was a public holiday, and he could easily think up some excuse to tack on another day's leave. And no one could accuse him of breaking any rules. He wouldn't be conducting an investigation, merely visiting a colleague on holiday and casually passing on some information. Who could find fault with that?

He looked up and beamed. 'These tomatoes are very good,' he said.

'Albuisson?' Zoe frowned, as Claude hung up the phone. 'What did he want? Is there something wrong at the house?'

'No,' said Claude, looking mildly puzzled. 'He says he needs to talk to me, and would I mind if he came down to see me tomorrow.'

'He wanted to come here? All this way? Why couldn't he just talk to you on the phone?'

'I don't know. He just said he'd prefer to see me in person.'

'Did he say what it's about?' said Zoe.

'It's some case he's investigating, but he wouldn't say any more than that on the phone. He said it would be better to wait until he gets here.'

'How mysterious,' said Moira. 'Any idea what it might be?'

'Not a clue.'

'It's probably just an excuse to get away from the office,' said Hugo. 'He fancies a couple of days off in Provence.'

'He's not really the sun-seeking type,' said Claude, 'for reasons which may become apparent when you see him.'

'Oh, he's coming, then, is he?' said Hugo. 'I'd have thought you'd have sent him away with a flea in his ear. I'm sure I wouldn't want any of my colleagues breaking into my holiday to talk about business.'

'Well, had he suggested I go back to St-Geraud to see him,

then I wouldn't have been quite so amenable. But if he wants to come here to see me, then let him. It won't hurt to spare him a couple of hours. And, I must admit, I'm curious to know what it's all about.'

'But, if he's coming here,' said Zoe, 'then who's going to feed our cat?'

11

Albuisson left home early, to take advantage of the cooler part of the day. His wife had prepared a packed lunch, to spare him the indignity of dining at a motorway café. It was mid-afternoon by the time he coasted off the *autoroute* at the Cavaillon exit. And, by God, it was hot; enervating, with the sun burning down on the windscreen. On the slower roads he lowered the windows to let in the air, but it made little difference.

He had told no one where he was going – not even Andrieu. As far as the rest of the world was concerned, he was off on a gastronomic pilgrimage. Well, why not? It was an explanation no one would question. He was well known to be a most enthusiastic member of a dining club which assembled at intervals to sample *haute cuisine*; as the club never met in the summer months, it was perfectly reasonable that he should indulge his passion elsewhere.

It wouldn't even be a lie. Michelin and Gault-Millau had disclosed a number of establishments worthy of his attention, all within easy driving distance of the Chavanacs' villa. There would be plenty of time to complete his mission and then find a place to stay and a suitable venue for the evening. And with only an early breakfast and a packed lunch inside him, he would be more than ready to do justice to an excellent dinner.

He turned off the main road, following the instructions Claude had given him over the telephone: right at the cross, over the little bridge, past the tall cypresses, left at the wayside shrine; and then not the first, not the second, but the third turning. There was a long, narrow track, that finally opened out into a driveway. He saw the stone walls of the villa glowing rich in the afternoon sun.

Oh, very nice, he thought. How much? Four or five weeks, high season: fifteen thousand, twenty thousand francs a week? By and large, he was not an avaricious man; he would settle for sufficiency. But there were times, when he encountered the likes of Claude Chavanac, that he felt it might be comforting to have a little more.

Mildly disgruntled, he walked up to the door and rang the bell.

'Oh, good, you're in,' said Andrieu. 'I was afraid you'd be out somewhere enjoying yourself, being as it's a holiday.'

'Chance'd be a fine thing,' said Chavanac's secretary, on the other end of the line. 'How did you get my home number?'

Andrieu said, vaguely: 'Office switchboard.'

'They're not supposed to give out our home numbers . . .'

'. . . except for official police business. I need your boss's home address. I have to feed his cat.'

'This is official police business?'

'Absolutely. Albuisson's gone off on some foodie jaunt, and left me with a set of keys and orders to feed this cat. What he didn't leave was the address.'

'Oh, all right.' She dictated it, and gave rough directions. 'It's not all that easy to find.'

He said, as though the thought had just occurred to him: 'Well, it sounds like I'll have to drive past your place on the way. So maybe I could pick you up and you could direct me. Then we could stop off for a drink or something on the way back.'

A long pause, then: 'Yes, I suppose so.'

Well, that was easier than expected, he thought, as he hung up and began to plan his next move. And she hadn't even asked how he knew where she lived.

'I see what you mean,' said Moira, in a muttered aside to Claude, as Albuisson's well-cushioned rear preceded him into the study. 'No one would mistake him for an open-air and fitness freak.'

Poor Albuisson. He was not built to wear summer casuals. But he had judged – correctly – that in his habitual business suit he would not blend seamlessly into the scenery of rural Provence in high summer. And so, anxious not to draw attention to himself, he had dressed in lightweight slacks and a casual shirt, both now crumpled and soggy. He looked like a pudding stuffed into a damp paper bag.

The rest of the family left him and Claude to their discussions, and repaired to the swimming-pool terrace. Presently, Fredy went indoors to get a cold drink, and came out again saying: 'Mum, Dad says can you go inside for a minute?'

'I expect they want tea and biscuits,' said Zoe. 'But there isn't a secretary to get it for them, and the poor things don't know what to do.'

In deference to the presence of a visitor, she covered her swimsuit with a brightly printed silk wrap, before going into the house. After an hour or so, Hugo remarked that she seemed to have been gone for rather a long time, but no one could be bothered to investigate.

In the study – fitted out more in the manner of a Scottish baronial hall than a Provençal farmhouse, with imposing fireplace and yards of matching books – Zoe paced back and forth by the window, as Albuisson delivered an abbreviated version of the story he had just relayed to Claude. He wished she would sit down. It was a struggle to concentrate, with the tropical colours of the silk – like the plumage of some exotic bird – flowing back and forth across his field of vision.

When he had finished, she turned to her husband.

'Could this really be happening?' she said. 'And could it really be Albert Brunet who's doing it?'

'I don't know.' Claude was oddly detached, as though discussing something that was happening to somebody else. 'I wouldn't have thought it was his style,' he said. 'If he was trying to get rid of me or frighten me off, I'd expect him to be more direct than that. And I've no idea what he might be afraid of. I haven't been rummaging through his dirty linen, nor did I ever intend to.'

'But did he know that? You've openly campaigned against corruption in the political establishment – and there was that article you wrote: "Swilling out the Augean stables", wasn't it? You can't make your intentions much clearer than that.'

'Yes, but it wasn't directed at Brunet. What's the point of gunning for him? He's out of it.'

'True, but he has friends who are still in it, right up to their grubby little ears. Maybe he knows that if you were to bring down one of them, he'd come tumbling down too.'

'But he's retired; he doesn't have a career to protect any longer.'

'Suppose it's not just a political thing? What if it's criminal? Then he'd have something to lose. Either way, it wouldn't do much for his elevated opinion of himself – or his vision of a comfortable retirement as a respected elder statesman. And, anyway, if he's not involved then why would he intervene to stop Georges investigating?'

'I didn't say we knew for certain it was Brunet who did that,' warned Albuisson.

'But you couldn't think who else it might have been,' said Claude.

Zoe said: 'So where do we go from here?'

'Well, I guess we've got a breathing space to make a few more discreet enquiries,' said Albuisson. 'You're probably safe enough while you're here in Provence.'

Zoe and Claude exchanged glances.

She said: 'Claude, have you told Georges about the rock?'

'I was just coming to that,' he said.

A decision had been made. Everyone should be told, including Fredy and Lucie. It was only fair, argued Zoe, that Hugo and Moira should know the score. Their safety could be at risk – whoever was targeting Claude, if that was indeed what was happening, showed no scruples about involving those around him; and they had Chiara to think of.

Albuisson was dubious about telling the older children.

'Won't it be very disturbing for them?' he said.

'Not half as disturbing as knowing something's wrong, and the grown-ups won't tell you what it is,' said Zoe. 'You know what kids' imaginations are like. If we try to protect them from worrying about this, they'll only dream up something far worse, and worry about that instead.'

So everyone was summoned to the study, while Chiara sat on the floor in the hallway outside, crayoning a portrait of Albuisson.

'Fucking hell,' said Hugo, when he had heard the story.

'Hugo, please!' said Moira. '*Pas devant les enfants.*'

'Moira,' said Zoe, gently, '*les enfants* speak better French than you do.'

'Fucking hell,' echoed Fredy, confident that, under the circumstances, no one was going to object. Lucie just went very quiet.

'I told Georges I thought it would be best if we went home,' Claude told Hugo and Moira. 'Then you and Chiara could stay on here and enjoy the rest of your holiday in peace. But Georges thinks we should stay. If the falling rock really is part of the same sequence of events, then whoever's doing this has followed us here from St-Geraud, which means he can just as easily follow us back again. We'd be no safer there than we are here – but *he* would. There, he can fade into the crowd. Here, he's more exposed; there's no crowd to fade into.'

'Good point,' said Hugo.

'But that doesn't mean you and Moira have to stay.'

'However,' Albuisson intervened, 'if he sees you leave, he may think you're on to him. That might frighten him off.'

'Isn't that what we want?' said Hugo.

'I'd say yes, if I thought he'd be frightened off for good; but I don't. He'd probably just go back to St-Geraud and lie in wait for another opportunity – and we'd have less chance of finding him.'

'But, wait a minute,' said Moira. She was looking at the copies of the newspaper ads, which Albuisson had spread on the table. 'This, this . . . person, whoever he is, he *wants* you to be on to him, doesn't he? Otherwise, why does he put ads in the newspaper to draw attention to the things he's done, and make quite sure that nobody mistakes them for accidents? When Claude didn't show any sign of having noticed the ads, he even had the nerve to send him copies of the newspapers!'

Albuisson nodded. 'I agree; he obviously wants Claude to know that something's happening. But I shouldn't think he wants to be caught. He's not giving anything away in these ads; they don't give any clues as to who's doing this, or why.'

'Isn't there any sort of message in the wording?' said Hugo.

'Oh, there are messages, but I don't think they tell us much,' said Claude.

Moira picked up the photocopies. '"Here's to the next time." That's the one after the car crash, isn't it? I suppose it means: don't think that's the end of it, there's more to come. Then, after the fire, it's "Don't you love the scent of pine?" That's something to do with burning pine logs, I suppose.'

'It's not just that,' said Zoe. 'Coffins are made of pine. There's an expression in French: if you say someone can smell the pine, it means they're close to death.'

'Oh, I see.' Moira shivered, despite the heat.

'What about this third one?' said Hugo. '"You can never replace the irreplaceable."'

'The books, I suppose,' said Claude. 'There were some rare books destroyed when my apartment was broken into, and they can't be replaced; that's the obvious allusion.'

'Presumably,' said Zoe, suddenly, 'if the falling rock was part of the sequence, there'll be a newspaper ad to follow that, too. That'll tell us if it was an accident or not.'

Moira was counting. 'It was three days ago.'

'The other ads appeared three or four days after the event,' said Albuisson. 'So if the pattern's repeated, there should be a new ad today or tomorrow. But where, I wonder? In *La Montagne*, like the others? Or here? What's the local paper?'

'*Le Provençal*,' said Zoe. 'We buy it in the village every morning. Today's copy should be lying around somewhere.'

'I'll go look for it,' said Fredy, seizing the chance to *do* something. But the newspaper could not be found.

'Never mind,' said Albuisson. 'If necessary, we can get hold of a copy from the publishers.'

'It's frustrating, though,' said Hugo. 'It would be nice to know, one way or another.'

Lucie spoke up for the first time. She tugged Zoe's arm, and whispered: 'Mummy, have you told the man about the pussycat?'

'I'm sorry, darling; what about the pussycat?'

'In the swimming pool.'

'Ah,' said Zoe slowly, understanding. 'You mean this nasty person might have drowned the cat, to frighten us? Now, there's a thought.'

And Moira said: 'There was that other thing, too, remember? When someone phoned up, pretending to be Claude, and cancelled our reservation at the restaurant.'

'Of course!' said Hugo. 'And they said we weren't coming because there'd been a death in the family. I thought that was weird at the time.'

'Tell me more,' said Albuisson; and, when they had done so, he thought for a moment, then said, with a sigh: 'Well, perhaps the newspapers will tell us. If these incidents were followed by advertisements, then we'll know they were part of the sequence. If not . . .'

'I've been keeping all the old newspapers,' said Moira.

'You have?' said Hugo. 'Why?'

'I was going to take them home. They'll be useful material for teaching Chiara to read French. I'll get them.'

And there they were, the advertisements.

Four days after the restaurant incident: 'C.C.: Just to let you know how I feel.'

And three days after the drowning: 'C.C.: I'll never forget you.'

It suddenly felt much cooler.

Zoe, compelled to break the tension, said briskly to Albuisson: 'Well, I don't suppose you're planning to drive back today, so you'll need a bed for the night.'

'No, no!' he said, hastily. 'I'll find a hotel. I wouldn't want to put you to any trouble.'

'Nonsense,' said Zoe. 'It's a public holiday; everywhere decent will be full. In any case, it's no trouble. This place is enormous; there's masses of space. There are bedrooms we haven't even found yet. It'll only take a few minutes to make up a bed. And you'll join us for dinner, of course.'

Albuisson's vision of gastronomic heaven dissolved like the Cheshire cat, leaving just a sickly smile. Heaven help him, he had fallen among Englishwomen. The prospect of an evening of boiled cabbage and stewed knitting stretched before him.

But his mother, whose influence had forged his love of food, had also instilled in him a rigid sense of manners. In the circumstances, it would not be polite to refuse an offer of hospitality. Meekly, he followed Zoe through the house, to be shown to his room.

'I expect you'd like to freshen up,' she said. 'There's a bathroom right opposite.'

She went off to find clean linen. Albuisson turned to see Chiara standing in the doorway, watching him warily. A strange child.

'Hello, little girl,' he said. He was never quite sure how to address small children.

She took a bold step into the room and held out her drawing-book for him to see. She had drawn a picture. She pointed at him, and then at the picture.

'Is that me?' he said.

She nodded.

He looked at the picture. It was a big yellow circle, with arms and legs sticking out like sausages, and two lopsided little pink eyes.

'It's a very good likeness,' he said.

12

Albuisson sat contented, nursing an elderly Armagnac. Things had not turned out as badly as he had feared. The dinner had been unexpectedly acceptable, some of it even quite accomplished. His compliments, not entirely concealing his surprise, were received with gracious amusement by his hostesses, who neglected to mention that most of the fare had come ready-prepared from the *traiteurs* and *pâtissiers* of Apt.

Now they were all contemplating their after-dinner drinks, in a hollow of silence occasionally filled with a burst of sudden conversation, that would just as suddenly subside. Everyone felt they should make an effort not to dwell on the subject that occupied their minds, but no one much wanted to talk about anything else.

In the end, it was Albuisson who said: 'Tell me about your neighbours. What are they like?'

Moira said, horrified: 'You think whoever's doing this could be someone from round here – somebody we *know*?'

'Well,' said Albuisson, 'if you think about what's happened here – assuming for the moment that the falling rock is part of it, though we can't be sure of that yet – you can see two things. First, whoever's doing this must be familiar with this house – and with your movements. He knew you'd booked a table at the restaurant, for example; he must have known that Claude was in the habit of sitting on the terrace where the rock fell, and presumably he also knew that the rest of you were going to be out that day. And, secondly, he couldn't have planned these things in advance, from a distance; he must have been close by all the time, waiting his chance. Take the day when the rock fell, for instance: when did you decide to make the outing to the Fontaine de Vaucluse?'

'It was just the night before, wasn't it?' said Hugo, glancing at Moira for confirmation. 'We discussed it over dinner, right here, where we are now.'

'And did you tell anyone else, anyone outside the family?'

Zoe said: 'There was no one here to tell. In the morning I went to the village shop, as usual, but I'm quite sure I didn't talk to anyone about our plans for the day.'

'Which means either that someone saw you leaving – but then he'd be taking a chance if he didn't know where you were going, or how long you'd be away – or that he overheard your conversation at the dinner table.'

Moira shuddered. 'You mean there could have been someone here, spying on us, eavesdropping?'

'He could even be here now,' said Zoe, bleakly.

'I don't want to think about it.'

'But you see what I'm getting at?' said Albuisson. 'We're talking about someone nearby. Someone who could come and go without arousing suspicion.'

'Practically everyone in the neighbourhood's been here at some time in the past couple of weeks,' said Claude. 'Think of all those people invited for aperitifs. And on the day of the *pétanque* match, we had the whole village wandering around the place. It wouldn't have been difficult for someone to work out the layout of the house, check the doors and windows for access . . .'

'But not so easy to do anything about it there and then,' said Albuisson, 'because there'd be too many other people around. He'd have had to come back some other time. Have you noticed anyone here when they shouldn't have been? Anything suspicious, prowlers . . .?'

Hugo said: 'I saw some kids, playing in the orchard.'

'When was that?'

'I don't remember; a few days ago. And then Moira saw them again, another time.'

'I never actually saw them,' said Moira. 'They must have heard me coming and hidden in the bushes, because by the time I got there, there was no one in sight. But they were still there; I could hear them. There was a sort of rustling in the undergrowth, and whispering.'

'Did you hear what was said?'

'Not clearly, no; I did catch a name, though. It was . . .' She bit her lip, concentrating, trying to remember. 'No, damn; it's gone.'

'Male or female?' said Albuisson.

'Male, I think; yes, I'm sure it was. Oh, if only I could remember what it was. Of course, I didn't think anything of it at the time; it didn't seem important. Otherwise it would have stuck in my mind.'

'And can you remember when it was that this happened?'

'I can,' said Zoe. 'It was the evening before we found the cat in the pool.'

'Jesus, does that mean . . .?' said Hugo.

'Let's not jump to conclusions just yet,' said Albuisson, cautiously. 'Let's just try and get all the information together. Has anything else like this happened?'

'What about the giant hamster?' said Fredy.

Zoe explained. Hugo suggested that Albuisson might like to investigate the roof-space there and then, and offered to fetch a torch; Albuisson, feeling rather too well-fed and wined for such exertions, expressed the view that it might be better left until daylight, and swiftly changed the subject.

'Let's think about who might be doing this,' he said. 'We'll exclude for the moment the permanent residents.'

'Why?' said Claude.

'Because, while they may be here now, it's unlikely they were also in St-Geraud in June and July.'

'You're sure it's the same person in both places?' said Hugo. 'I mean, this politician you mentioned, what's his name, Brunet: you thought he might be responsible for what was going on in St-Geraud. But, obviously, he's not here; you said you saw him at his home, a couple of days ago.'

'If it is Brunet, I never imagined for one minute he'd be doing his own dirty work,' said Albuisson. 'He couldn't have damaged Claude's car in St-Flour, for a start, because he was very visibly present right through the lunch. No, he'd get someone else to do it, one way or another.'

'Then why not more than one person?' suggested Zoe. 'One in St-Geraud, a different one here.'

'Possible, but is it likely? Involving one person in something like this is risky enough. Brunet's a cautious man; Auvergnat through and through. I doubt if he'd take the risk twice – even if he could find two people willing to do it.'

'So we're looking at the temporary residents, then,' said Claude. 'Presumably someone pretending to be here on holiday. What about the foreigners? It's like the United Nations here – Germans, Dutch, Swiss, Belgians, British. Do we rule them out, too?'

'Yes, I think so, for the time being,' said Albuisson. 'Unless, of course . . . were you speaking English when you discussed the trip to the Fontaine de Vaucluse?'

'No,' said Fredy, with a sullen glance at Moira. 'We're not allowed to speak English during dinner.'

'In that case, let's concentrate on the French,' said Albuisson.

'Well, that narrows it down,' said Zoe. 'There's the Rocards; they're from Paris. And that nice old couple from Orléans – I think their name is Masson; and the Newlyweds.'

'Don't forget the Hippopotamus,' said Claude.

Albuisson sighed deeply. First, a giant hamster; now a hippopotamus; what next?

'And her lunch,' added Hugo.

'They're from Paris, too,' said Zoe. 'Her name's de Sousa; I don't know about him.'

'What about these Newlyweds?' said Albuisson. 'What are they called?'

Everyone looked blank.

'No one calls them anything but the Newlyweds,' said Moira.

'We can ask in the village,' said Zoe. 'Someone must know.'

'Well, out of that lot,' said Albuisson, 'who would you say are the most likely suspects?'

'If we're thinking of someone hired by Brunet, then I'd go for the Newlyweds,' said Hugo. 'They're young, so they're probably more likely than the others to do something like this for money. And they're fit; they'd be capable of climbing on the roof to push the rock off – I can't see the Hippo doing that, or the old couple.'

'And, anyway, the husband of the old couple was having heart surgery at the time when things were happening in St-Geraud,' said Moira, 'so I think we have to count them out.'

'Unfortunately' said Zoe, 'I think we have to rule out the Newlyweds, too. Because on the day the rock fell, they weren't here; they were at the Fontaine de Vaucluse, just like the rest of us.'

Zoe had taken the children to bed. They had been fending off sleep, half-excited by the goings-on, half-afraid to be alone in the dark; suddenly, thoughts of giant hamsters no longer seemed so entertaining. But finally, drowsiness had got the better of them.

Lucy fell asleep as soon as her head hit the pillow; Zoe stayed with Fredy, ignoring his protestations of self-sufficiency, until he too drifted into dozy oblivion. With the two of them taken care of, she looked in on Chiara. Unaffected by the day's events, and happily put to bed hours ago, now she lay peacefully sleeping, curled up sideways across the bed and clutching a moth-eaten rabbit.

Zoe yearned for such simple comforts. She felt very tired. Going into the nearest bathroom, she peered in the mirror. There were shadows beneath her eyes. She splashed her face with cold water, and reached for a towel; it was then that she saw the missing newspaper.

She took it to show the others.

'It had fallen down behind the laundry basket,' she said. 'Someone must have taken it to read in the loo.'

'Oops,' said Hugo. 'Sorry. I forgot.'

'Have you looked at the ads?' said Claude, not sure if he wanted to hear the answer.

Zoe shook her head. 'I couldn't face it.' She handed the newspaper to Albuisson. 'Here. You do it.'

Albuisson shifted his chair into the light. He opened the paper. Nobody spoke. After a time, he looked up.

'Is it there?' said Zoe.

He nodded.

'What does it say?' asked Hugo.

'It says "C.C.: The last ten years – I owe it all to you."'

Albuisson dreamed of hippopotami and hamsters, and woke, hot and airless, in the dark before dawn. He lay engulfed in the deep rural silence that seems louder than noise, thinking: What now? That last newspaper ad had thrown everything up in the air.

Ten years.

What did that mean?

What it meant – if it were true; if it meant anything at all – was that Albert Brunet was probably not their man. A decade ago, Claude had never met him; barely knew of him – at least, no more than any other young man might know of a middle-aged, middle-rank, behind-the-scenes politician – which was all that Brunet was, in those days. Certainly, Claude had never, to his knowledge, crossed Brunet's path in any way that might have changed the man's life for the next ten years.

Of course, the ad could be a decoy, intended to provoke precisely these conclusions. It was, Albuisson calculated, the first to appear since Brunet had become aware of his enquiries. It could have been placed deliberately, to throw him off the trail.

But suppose it wasn't, he had said to Claude. Suppose it was the real thing. What then? What were you doing ten years ago?

Claude had poured himself a rather large cognac.

They were in Paris, he had said, eventually. It was their last year there. Zoe was pregnant. They didn't want to raise kids in a flat in the sixteenth; they were making plans to move out of the city.

And Zoe had said: 'You were working on the Grissot case for most of that year, weren't you?'

'What was that?' Albuisson asked.

Claude said: 'Fraud and embezzlement. One of those long drawn-out trials, complicated – they always are, cases like that. A businessman called Grissot had accused his lawyers of misappropriating funds that belonged to him. It caused quite a scandal at the time. It was an old-established law firm, ultra-respectable. Seven of the partners were charged – and three of them happened to be old colleagues of mine; we were students together. It wasn't my usual kind of case, but they asked me to represent them, so I did.'

'Were they guilty as charged?'

Claude pursed his lips, considering, ever the lawyer. 'I suppose the answer is yes and no. They did misuse money that belonged to the client – but they never intended to keep it. What happened was that Grissot was bidding to buy a company, and part of the deal required him to lodge a large sum of money with his lawyers, by way of a deposit. They'd worked out a scam, whereby they'd briefly divert funds out of the client account, and use it to play the money markets. The money was only out of the account for a matter of hours – usually overnight; they'd trade on the New York market, make a quick profit, and the money would be back before anybody noticed it had gone. They'd done it before, with other clients' money, and got away with it. But on this occasion, Grissot decided to call on his funds overnight, and . . . well, you can imagine. Pandemonium.'

'What were the verdicts?'

'They were all found guilty, except for one of the three that I was defending, a man by the name of Laurent Jouvet. He knew what was going on, but he wasn't directly involved – well, not in this particular instance. He was guilty by omission for not reporting it, naturally; but there were senior partners involved, and he was just a junior, so he wasn't in a strong position to blow the whistle. At least, that was our defence.'

'And the sentences, for the others?'

'One of my clients, Richard Dullin, got five years – they held him responsible for thinking up the idea in the first place. The other one, Jean-Michel Artaud, he just went along for the ride;

they gave him eighteen months. The rest of them got two or three years; I don't remember the details.'

'What became of them all?'

'I don't know. We left Paris not long after the trial was over, and I lost touch with them. I did meet up with Jouvet a few times; we'd have lunch now and then, if I was in Paris on business. He told me Dullin got religion while he was inside, and Artaud had a bad time; his wife divorced him, took the kids and went running home to mother. I don't know what happened to him after that; Jouvet might know.'

'Would you know how to contact him?'

'I've got an address and phone number – not here; it's in a file in my office. I don't know if it's still valid; I haven't seen him for several years. But if you want it, ask Martine, my secretary. She should be able to find it.'

Albuisson could deal with that once he got back to St-Geraud; get Andrieu on to it. It might be a profitable line of enquiry. Dullin and Artaud had been successful young lawyers, with promising careers ahead of them; a prison sentence, even a short one, must have had a dramatic effect on their lives. One of them at least had lost his wife and children because of it, and there was undoubtedly more to it than that. Sufficient incentive for one – or even both? – of them to seek revenge against the man who had failed to clear their names in court?

But if they were responsible, where were they?

It was possible, he supposed, that they might be acting by proxy, using someone else to do the dirty work. But that didn't feel right. If it were Brunet, then yes: nothing odd about hiring someone to put the frighteners on. But if the motive was revenge, then weren't you more likely to want the satisfaction of doing it yourself? Wasn't that the whole point?

Yet neither of them was visibly at large in the neighbourhood. Even if they'd changed so radically in appearance that Claude had failed to recognize them, there seemed to be no one here to fit the bill. If they were all students together, they'd presumably be about the same age as Claude – but the only local candidate in that category was Philippe Rocard, and he had been Claude's neighbour, not his client.

So maybe this was nothing to do with the fraud case. Maybe something else had happened ten years ago, something perhaps so trivial that Claude didn't even remember it – but for someone else it had been a life-shattering event.

The whole thing was wide open. One could possibly rule out the so-called Newlyweds: they were too young – ten years ago they were just children; they were little more than that even now – and they had been seen, more than once, at the Fontaine de Vaucluse on the day of the falling rock. But apart from that, everyone in the neighbourhood now looked like a potential suspect. And there was still a question mark over Albert Brunet.

It was getting light already. He felt as though he had hardly slept, and there seemed little chance that sleep would come now. He lay restless, thinking, for another half-hour, ideas pursuing each other round his mind in tedious circles, and then he decided to call it a night, and got up.

13

Coming downstairs in the early morning, Zoe found Albuisson already up and dressed and looking a trifle peckish.

'I'm just off to the village to get the bread for breakfast,' she said, reassuringly.

'Do you mind if I come with you?' It might be a good idea to take a look around, he thought.

'Please do.'

She tried to imagine Albuisson riding a bicycle. Perhaps not. Better take the car. *En route,* she pointed out the Hippopotamus's villa, across the vineyards and just visible through the trees.

'What about the other people you mentioned?' said Albuisson. 'Where are they staying?'

'The Massons' place is a few kilometres further west,' she said, 'and the Rocards are in one of those new villas you can see up ahead, on the hillside above the village. The Newlyweds are staying in the village itself; I'm not sure exactly where. That's their motor bike, over there,' she added, as she drove into the square and parked arbitrarily.

'I'll wait here,' said Albuisson.

'What shall I say if anyone asks who you are?'

'Best not to say I'm a policeman, I think. Say, er . . . why don't you say I'm Claude's doctor, visiting to give him a check-up.'

'Yes, that sounds plausible,' she said.

As she walked up the hill towards the *alimentation générale*, he strolled around the square, making mental notes. He checked out the motor bike: a big, high-powered German model, lovingly cared for. He noted its *matriculation* and, squinting more closely at the plate, the name of the dealer who had supplied it: Ets Roland, Limoges.

Behind the bike was a big, showy, white Mercedes with a Paris registration. He walked past it slowly, giving it the once-over, and as he did so, a short, slight young man came out of the shop and headed towards the car. Albuisson wished him good morning.

The young man looked slightly startled, then nodded curtly and climbed into the car; he could barely see over the steering wheel. With a haste that seemed out of proportion to the quiet village morning, he revved the engine hard and drove off with squealing tyres in a cloud of dust.

It was a nervous, guilty reaction; Albuisson was instantly suspicious. Then he told himself to ease off. A Paris-registered car, remember; they all behave like that in Paris. He was in danger of becoming paranoid, seeing suspects everywhere, and that would not do. Being over-suspicious was just as dangerous in its way as being excessively trusting.

He saw Zoe coming out of the shop in the company of a couple who, from the descriptions he had already been given, he took to be Philippe and Joelle Rocard. They chatted for a moment or two, then the couple headed off up the hill and Zoe came back down to the square.

'Who's the midget in the white Mercedes?' Albuisson asked her, as they drove back to the villa.

'That's what Hugo calls the Hippopotamus's lunch.'

Bravely, he ventured to enquire: 'Why is that?'

'There's a South Sea island called Tonga,' said Zoe, 'and the natives were supposed to have been cannibals at one time. So when the Queen of Tonga – who was enormous – turned up at Queen Elizabeth's coronation with a tiny little man sitting beside her, some wit suggested that he was her packed lunch. Hugo was a schoolboy at the time, so naturally he thought this was hilarious.'

'I see,' said Albuisson, little the wiser. The English sense of humour completely eluded him.

At the villa, over breakfast, Moira cleared her throat and made an announcement. 'Hugo and I', she said, 'have been talking things over, and we've decided to stay. Georges is quite right: if we change our plans, we may frighten off whoever's doing all these awful things, and make them more difficult to track down. We know there's an element of risk – but, let's face it, it's Claude they're after, not us. And there's safety in numbers. The more of us there are around the house, the fewer chances there are for someone to get in. And, well, we're family, and families should stick together.'

'And anyway,' said Hugo, jovially, 'we listened to the weather report on the radio, and it's pissing down at home.'

Albuisson was preparing to leave, when Claude cornered him, away from the others.

'Before you go,' he said, 'just one more thing.'

'Yes?' said Albuisson.

'Let's go to the study.'

When they got there, Claude closed the door firmly behind him.

'There's something I didn't mention last night,' he said. 'I didn't want to say it in front of the others.'

Albuisson waited.

'About ten years ago,' said Claude, 'I had an affair with Philippe Rocard's wife.'

'Ah,' said Albuisson, exhaling slowly.

'We were neighbours, as you know. That's all there was to it, really. It wasn't that I was particularly attracted to her; to be honest, I didn't even like her very much. It was just that she was there. Zoe never knew about it; that's why I didn't want to mention it last night.'

'What about the woman's husband? Did he know?'

'She said not. She always insisted he didn't have even the slightest suspicion – and, at the time, I took her word for it.

Now, I begin to wonder. Perhaps he did know. He's not with her now, so, obviously, something happened to their marriage – but I don't know what, or when, or whether it had anything to do with our relationship.'

'And this, um, relationship: how did it end?'

'It just came to a natural conclusion when Zoe and I moved out of Paris.'

'Was there any further contact after that – phone calls, letters? Did you meet this woman when you went to Paris on business?'

'No. I never saw her again. Frankly, I was glad it was over. I certainly made no attempt to keep in touch.'

'And she never tried to contact you?'

'Not that I know of.'

Albuisson softly drummed his fingers on the arm of his chair. Philippe Rocard; he pictured him as he had seen him this morning outside the village shop, amiably chatting with Zoe, his arm around his wife. A bitter, twisted, vengeful man? He certainly didn't look the part.

But then, he wouldn't, would he? Not if he had any sense. In St-Geraud, he could hide; but here in Provence, he would know that, if he was to get close to the Chavanacs, he would be all too visible. And they would be sure to recognize him. So, if he couldn't use concealment, he would have to resort to camouflage. Disguise himself as a happy, friendly soul with a pretty young wife. Was she even his wife? Or just another part of the deception? Something else for Andrieu to look into.

He said, tentatively, to Claude: 'Look, I can quite understand why you wouldn't want to tell Zoe about this, but don't you think you should? If Philippe Rocard is a serious suspect, shouldn't she be warned?'

He expected argument, but Claude was unexpectedly subdued: 'Yes, you're absolutely right. I just can't bring myself to tell her.'

'Would it come as that much of a shock to her? Surely she knows . . .'

'. . . what a shit I am? Yes, of course she does – now. But back then, in Paris, you see, we were the golden couple – the perfect marriage, the envy of all our friends. We weren't going to be like everyone else . . . well, you know how it is.' He showed a faint, rueful smile.

'So what went wrong?'

'The usual things. We got older. We had children. That's what makes the difference. You think you've broken out from where you came from, but children pull you back. You revert to type. I used to look at my father and his friends and convince myself I'd never be like that . . . you know, within hours of his wedding, my father was in bed with his mistress. My mother just put on a pair of blinkers, and got on with running the family. But then, she came from the same mould as he did; she knew what to expect. She was there for duty, the mistress was for pleasure. Zoe doesn't see things quite like that.'

A sublime understatement, thought Albuisson.

'Nor do I,' said Claude, 'if I think about it. But I didn't think about it; I just let it happen. Time goes by, I look in the mirror and see my father. Zoe didn't see it, though, not to begin with; she thinks the rot set in much later than it did.'

'But now that she does know, what difference would it make if she found out about you and Rocard's wife?'

'I guess it's just that she knows I'm a shit, but she doesn't know how big a shit I am. If she knew that even when everything seemed fine, it wasn't; that even when I seemed like a devoted husband and father-to-be, I was in our neighbour's apartment, screwing his wife, well . . . do you see what I mean?'

Albuisson nodded. He heard himself saying, against his better judgement: 'All right. We'll say nothing for the moment. I'll make some enquiries about Rocard – it may be we can rule him out, in which case there's no need for any more to be said. But if the enquiries confirm our suspicions, then I'm afraid . . .'

'Let's worry about that when the time comes,' said Claude. And then, as an afterthought: 'Thanks.'

It was evening when Albuisson eventually got home, and all he'd had for lunch was a small and undistinguished sandwich. Luckily, his wife had anticipated this possibility.

'Your mother rang,' she said, dishing out a generous portion of *ris de veau* in a good white wine sauce, one of his particular favourites. 'And that young policeman, what's his name?'

'Andrieu?'

'Yes, him. Cheeky so-and-so, isn't he?' Andrieu had addressed her familiarly as 'Madame A', and made some joke about her husband having left her for another cook, which she had not considered funny.

'Did he leave a message?'

'He said he had information on someone called Philippe Rocard, but it would wait until tomorrow.'

'Good,' said Albuisson, reluctant to interrupt his meal.

It had been a long day. First, there had been the inspection of the roof-space at the Chavanacs' villa: an undignified episode, in which he had almost got stuck in a very small trapdoor (like Pooh Bear wedged in a window, Hugo said later).

And once he was up there, he had seen nothing of interest, just a lot of dust and a few mouse droppings and pistachio shells. But he had established that from there one could hear very clearly people speaking in the rooms below, and that there was a further trapdoor giving access to the roof itself. So someone could have been up there, hiding, eavesdropping – and then climbing out on to the tiles to tip the rock over the edge to the terrace below.

But Claude had not been there. Did the perpetrator know that, or had he simply not seen that the sun lounger was empty? It was easily visible now, through the hole that the rock had smashed in the trellis. But, at the time, the thick cover of vine would have obscured the view, so that someone crouching on the roof – taking care not to be spotted himself – might have been unable to see clearly if the lounger were occupied or not. Had the intention been to do harm, believing Claude to be there – or merely to create fear, knowing that he wasn't? Verdict: undecided.

After that, there was the private conversation with Claude. And then, as he was on the point of leaving, someone had remembered photographs taken at the *pétanque* match – potentially useful for identification of most of the local residents – and there had been a further delay while the rolls of exposed film were found.

Finally, on the way home, he had driven via Avignon, and called at the local office of the newspaper, *Le Provençal*. He was quite out of order, not at all his usual style – outside his own territory, and no liaison with the local police. But he wanted the thing done quickly, while there was a chance that the paperwork for the most recent ad might still be on the premises.

The newspaper staff were accommodating, checking their records to find what he wanted. As he had fully expected, the story was much the same as it had been for *La Montagne*. Each ad had come in to a different office – one at Marseille, one at Aix, one at Avignon; the payments were in cash; there were no names or addresses on file. But his luck was in; the ad in yesterday's paper had come in to the Avignon office and, as he had hoped, they still had the original request.

It was a single sheet of paper, plain white, 80 grams; the kind of commonplace stationery you would find in any office throughout the country. He held it up to the light; no watermark. It was stamped with the date of receipt – two days ago – but there was no indication of how it had arrived, and the envelope had been discarded.

The text had been produced, he would guess, on a laser or bubblejet printer – compatible with the description given by the witness at *La Montagne*, who had seen what he thought might have been the order for one of the earlier ads. Again, it was the kind of thing that might have come from any modern office – although how would someone stuck in the Provençal countryside gain access to an office?

The letter was short and direct. It read: 'Please insert the following advertisement in the Personal section in tomorrow's edition of your newspaper. Lineage payment is enclosed.' The wording of the ad was just as it had appeared in print. There was no signature but, at the top of the page, there was a name and address: M. P. Bonnard, 12 rue Lamartin, 13300 Salon-de-Provence.

Naturally, the Salon street directory revealed that there was no such address.

Zoe woke, and the bed was empty beside her. A faint, pale light was gathering by the window; the bright red digits of the bedside clock told her it was five thirty-five. Assuming that Claude had gone to the bathroom, she rolled over and dozed, but when she woke again, ten minutes had passed and he was still not there.

She sat up, mildly anxious. Claude was not by habit an early riser. Wrapping herself in a dressing-gown, she went in search, and found him outside on the balcony, watching the dawn. The land was drawn in pastels, the Luberon a lazy grey mist. In a field there were figures already moving, stooping to pick tomatoes and aubergines before the heat of the day.

'I couldn't sleep,' he said.

'What's the matter?'

'This damn leg hurts, that's all.'

But it wasn't all; that was obvious.

'Are you scared?' she said.

'I suppose I should be, but no – I was just making a mental list of all the people who might possibly have any kind of grievance against me.'

'And?'

'And it's a hell of a long list. I know I've never gone out of my way to make myself universally loved, but I hadn't realized I'd made quite so many enemies.'

'Even saints make enemies.'

'Nevertheless, it's a salutary thought, when you consider all the people who must really hate you – and not without reason. And there must be plenty more who wish, on the whole, they'd never met me. Like you, for example. Don't you ever wish you'd married someone else?'

'Well, I did consider Harrison Ford at one time, but . . .'

'Be serious.'

'Life is difficult enough without being serious, especially at six o'clock in the morning. Why don't you stop brooding and come back to bed?'

Claude smiled for the first time.

'What can we do there that we can't do here?' he said.

14

'So it wasn't Brunet after all?' said Andrieu, flicking through the newspapers Albuisson had brought back from Provence.

'Doesn't look like it, does it?'

'Then why did he get the investigation stopped?'

'Force of habit, probably,' said Albuisson. He'd had plenty of time to think it through on the journey home. 'It's the kind of thing that politicians do. They pull strings – not necessarily because they have to; they do it just because they can.'

'What about the staff at the hotel in St-Flour? Why were they lying?'

'We don't know that they were. It was just a hunch. Maybe we were trying too hard to convince ourselves that there was something going on.'

Andrieu was sceptical. But he wasn't about to argue the point; he was just glad that the case was on the move again, even if it was now heading in a totally different direction.

It was all official now – with this new information from Provence, even Parrilaud could hardly object. Not that official status had conferred any additional manpower; at this time of year, there was no one to spare. And with the forensic labs also running on empty, there was little hope of an early response to the sheet of paper that Albuisson had sent for analysis; they still hadn't come up with a report on the lighter he'd found in Chavanac's garden, and they'd had that for over a week.

But now at least he could stop pussyfooting around and get on with something positive. Well, fairly positive. Albuisson had set the priority: to trace Philippe Rocard's ex-wife.

'What about the other possibilities?' Andrieu had asked. 'Like the people connected with the fraud case?'

'One thing at a time. We don't have the resources for parallel enquiries. And right now, Rocard's number one on the list. There's the timing – ten years, that's exactly how long it is since his wife's affair; plus the fact that he's right there in Provence, in the same tiny village as the Chavanacs – it takes some imagination to see that as just coincidence.'

'Then why not get him in for questioning?' Andrieu, as ever, favoured the direct approach.

'Because judges can be perversely imaginative. The evidence at the moment is circumstantial at best; unless he just rolls over and confesses, which I doubt, it won't stick. We need something a bit more solid. And until we've got it, I don't want Rocard alerted to the fact that we're on to him. Look what happened with Brunet.'

'But Brunet has friends in high places. Rocard doesn't. What could he do to us?'

'We don't know that he doesn't have influential friends – we don't know anything about him, yet. And even if he doesn't, we'd still be sending him warning signals; we'd be giving him a chance to cover his tracks. If he thinks he's getting away with it, he may be careless; that's what we want. So we don't let him know he's under suspicion; we don't even ask him for his ex-wife's address. Is that quite clear? We take the circuitous route. It may take a little longer, but there's a better chance of arriving where we want to be.'

'So how do we find this woman?'

'Start with Chavanac's files. He can't remember the name of the company she worked for when he knew her, but he thinks he may have the address on a file in his office. With luck, she might still be working there – or, if not, her employers may know where she moved on to. So you might like to pay another call on that secretary of his.'

Indeed I might, thought Andrieu.

'This is the file,' said Martine, taking down a long, red oblong box from a shelf behind her desk. The box pulled out like a drawer, and inside were crammed hundreds of index cards – different colours, some typed and some handwritten, most of them battered and dog-eared.

'They're all in here,' she said, 'all his contacts, going back years. I keep offering to put it all on the computer; it'd make life much easier. But he won't have it. He likes his cards.' She riffled through the Rs. 'Here we are: Rocard, Francine. Who is she?'

Andrieu was cagey – partly because Albuisson had warned him not to talk about the case to anyone, but mainly to keep Martine guessing. A sense of mystery, he thought, of knowledge too important to be divulged, would do his image no harm at all. 'Just someone your boss knew ten years ago,' he said.

She was looking at the adjacent card. 'There's another one here: Philippe Rocard. Do you want him as well?'

'Ah, yes.' That was an unexpected bonus.

For Francine Rocard there was a Paris phone number, with extension, and the name of a company: Jaillot Frères; no address. Her ex-husband's card had two numbers; after the first one, in brackets, it said 'apt' – which presumably meant 'apartment' – and after the second, 'BDC'. Could that be the name of a company?

Martine photocopied the cards, and he folded the copy and stuck it in his wallet. She put the cards back in the box. Should he ask if she was free tonight, he wondered. Maybe this time they could go to the cinema. No; mustn't seem too eager. Perhaps he'd call her later.

'Right, then, I'll be off,' he said.

Albuisson squinted at the photocopy.

'Jaillot Frères?' He frowned. 'That rings a bell. Of course, if this is ten years old, it'll be out of date. They've changed all the phone numbers since then.'

'I know,' said Andrieu, tapping at his keyboard. 'That's why I'm checking on Minitel, to see if I can find a current number for this company – assuming it still exists. Aha! Here it is.'

'Of course!' Albuisson snapped his fingers. 'I knew the name was familiar. They're wine merchants.'

Of course, thought Andrieu, who knew little of such things. He generally bought wine in shrink-wrapped packs at Leclerc, three bottles for twenty francs; maybe twenty-five, for special occasions.

He lifted the phone and dialled the number. A haughty female voice responded.

'Francine Rocard? No, we have no one of that name here.'

'We know she worked there some years ago,' he said. 'Do you keep details of former staff?'

'Well, I expect the personnel manager does, but he's on holiday and his files are locked.'

Andrieu's spirits sank.

'Oh, wait a minute,' the woman said.

And rose again.

'Of course. You mean Francine *Julien*. Rocard was her name before she got married again.'

'Ah! And does she still work there?'

'No. She transferred to our Bordeaux branch years ago. The phone number? Yes, certainly.'

The woman who answered the phone at the Bordeaux branch of Jaillot Frères sounded identical to her Paris counterpart.

'Madame Julien? I'm sorry, she's on holiday.'

'Shit,' said Andrieu. 'You don't happen to know where, do you?'

'I'm afraid it's not company policy to give that sort of information over the phone.'

'This is the police,' he said, officiously. 'We need to contact her urgently. It's a – um – family matter.'

'Oh dear.' The woman was wavering. 'But how do I know you really are the police?'

He sighed. 'My name's Andrieu,' he said. 'St-Geraud police headquarters, Cantal. You can look up the number on Minitel. I'll hang up, you call me back. Then you'll know I'm who I say I am. Okay?'

He put down the handset. In a few minutes the phone rang.

'Satisfied?' he said.

'Um, I suppose so.' The tone of the woman's voice said she still wasn't happy about it, but nevertheless she told him what he wanted to know.

'Gordes?' said Albuisson. 'She's on holiday in Gordes?'

'Apparently she goes there every year,' said Andrieu, 'for some arty-farty festival.'

'But that's in the same area as the Chavanacs,' said Albuisson, crossly. He'd been there just the day before yesterday; if only he'd known. 'Do we have any idea where she's staying?'

'Yes, she'd given her company the name of her hotel, in case anyone needed to contact her in an emergency.'

'Then I suppose there's nothing for it but another trip to Provence.' Albuisson viewed the prospect with little enthusiasm.

'I could go, if you like,' said Andrieu, hopefully.

'Yes, I suppose you could,' said Albuisson. He immediately wished he hadn't; but by then it was too late.

Andrieu roared down the A7 with total disregard for common-sense or traffic regulations. Luckily, at four thirty in the morning, there was virtually no other traffic on the road.

He was feeling pretty pleased with himself. First, he'd persuaded Albuisson that he could be trusted to handle Francine Rocard on his own, with due tact and diplomacy – and not before time; he was sick of being treated like an unreliable kid.

And then, in a clever bit of detective work, he'd decoded the information on Philippe Rocard. BDC had turned out to be a small, Paris-based computer company, subsequently taken over and rechristened by its new American owners. After an hour of telephone calls, he had finally tracked down the new company, and discovered with glee that Philippe Rocard still worked there.

'He's now their sales manager,' he had told Albuisson, smugly. 'And guess what? In June and July this year, he was running a promotional roadshow in the Massif Central.'

'You mean he would have been in St-Geraud?'

'Not all the time; they were moving from town to town. But he was here around the time of the fire at Chavanac's house, and he wasn't far away when the other incidents occurred.'

Albuisson frowned suspiciously. 'How did you find this out? Have you been talking to his colleagues? We don't want them warning him that the police are after him.'

'I'm not that dumb,' said Andrieu, all injured innocence. 'I came on like a potential customer; told them I'd like to see their stuff, and were any of their salespeople likely to be in this area in the near future? And they said, well, that's a real shame, because we've been targeting your area, and our sales team were there just a few weeks ago; we've stopped for the summer now, but maybe you can pick up one of our shows in the autumn. So I got them to fax me their roadshow schedule.'

'You had them send it here?'

'It's just a telephone number,' said Andrieu. 'They don't know it's police. Even if they did, it's no problem; the police buy computers, don't they?'

Albuisson couldn't argue with that; the place was full of the damn things.

'Anyway, this list arrived, and it had all the roadshow dates for the year – past as well as future. And you can see,' – Andrieu slid the list across the desk – 'even when Rocard wasn't actually here, he was within an hour or two's drive on the relevant dates.'

So now, with increasing confidence that Rocard was their man, Andrieu was speeding towards Provence and an interview with his former wife. Good thing he hadn't, after all, fixed a date with Martine, or he'd have had to cancel it. He'd planned the trip carefully, going home early to snatch some sleep and setting the alarm for the early hours, so that he could be at Francine Julien's hotel by breakfast time, catch her before she went out for the day. No problem.

'. . . just disappeared,' Madame P was saying to the little old lady at the front of the queue, as Zoe came into the shop. 'Gone! Pouf! Just like that. It was my sister's girl Suzanne – you know, the one with the squint; she was going round there every day to do the cleaning. Well, yesterday morning she turned up as usual, and the place was all locked up, shutters closed, no sign of life. No car, nothing.

'Suzanne had a key, of course, she let herself in, and there on the kitchen table there was an envelope with her name on it. So she opened it, and there was money inside, and a note saying how they'd had to go back to Paris at short notice – no explanation or anything; and here was her wages for the rest of the month – plus a bit extra for the inconvenience. Some inconvenience – getting paid over the odds for doing nothing. Right up her street, that is; she's always been a lazy little so-and-so.'

'Well!' said the little old lady. 'What a thing, dashing off like that, without a word to anyone. I wonder why.'

'What are they talking about?' Zoe whispered to the woman just ahead of her in the queue. 'Who's disappeared?'

'It's that what's-her-name,' the woman said. 'The big fat woman, you know – Madame de Sousa.'

15

The woman was tall, with smooth fair hair and long legs; the man was shorter and thicker, with a prissy little mouth and expensive sun-glasses. They looked, thought Andrieu, exactly the kind of people who would go to arts festivals.

The waiter had pointed them out to him as they came down for breakfast. There were tables arranged around a tree-shaded courtyard; they settled themselves at one in the corner, by the wall. Andrieu hung back until the waiter had brought their order, and then introduced himself.

He didn't come on heavy; he was the soul of discretion. Albuisson would have been proud of him. Even so, the man instantly took umbrage – he was that type, the ones you can't ask the time of day without them ranting about their rights and demanding to know the name of your superior. But the woman was all right, in a condescending sort of way.

'He's only doing his job, Charles,' she said. 'I don't mind answering a few questions. It's not going to take all day, is it?'

'I shouldn't think so,' said Andrieu.

'Well, get on with it, then,' the man said, sulkily.

'Not here, if you don't mind, M'sieur Julien. I'd like to talk to your wife in private. I've spoken to the manager; he says we can use his office.'

'Oh, you've spoken to the manager, have you? I suppose now he thinks we're common criminals; he'll be asking us to pay in advance, I expect, in case we run off without settling the bill. And just what do you have to say to my wife that you can't say in front of me?'

It's not so much what I might say to her, thought Andrieu, as what she might say to me. Maybe Charles Julien already knew about his wife's extra-marital affairs; but then again, maybe he didn't.

'I'm sorry, sir; it's a question of confidentiality,' he said.

'This is outrageous! If my wife wants me to be there . . .'

'Does she?'

They both looked at her.

'Oh, for heaven's sake, Charles,' she said, 'if he wants to talk to me alone, then let him.'

Andrieu left them to finish their breakfast, and then Francine Julien accompanied him to the manager's office, while her husband went up to their room with a face like a thunderstorm.

She looked around and said: 'Where would you like me to sit?'

'Wherever you like.'

She chose an upright chair by the desk, and Andrieu immediately recognized his mistake. He wanted her to feel at ease; didn't want to intimidate by standing over her or taking the manager's imposing leather swivel chair behind the desk. But the only other option was a squashy pink sofa. When he sat, he sank deep into the cushions, so that she was looking down on him; he could see right up her skirt. She lit an American cigarette and crossed her legs. He blinked.

'What's all this about?' she said.

Andrieu swallowed hard. 'Do you remember a man named Claude Chavanac?'

That took the edge off her cool. She didn't know what to say. She tried to create the illusion that she was trawling her memory, then said, offhandedly: 'Er . . . yes. When I lived in Paris, years ago, he was a neighbour, lived in the same building.'

'You had an affair with him, didn't you?'

'Who told you that?'

'He did.' He paused a moment, to let that sink in. She took short, nervous drags on her cigarette. 'And at the time,' he said, 'you were married to a man named Philippe Rocard.'

'You have been doing your homework, haven't you? Been talking to Philippe, too?'

'Not yet. I wanted to talk to you first, hear your side of the story.'

She stubbed out her cigarette, half-smoked, and recrossed her legs in the opposite direction. I do wish she wouldn't do that, Andrieu thought.

'All right,' she confessed. 'I had an affair with Claude.'

'Did your husband know about it? Your first husband, I mean.'

'Not at the time, no. We were very discreet.'

'You say he didn't know at the time. Does this imply he found out later?'

'Yes.'

'How did that happen?'

She lit another cigarette.

'Look, how far is all this going to go? I mean, if I tell you . . .'

'No further than necessary.'

She hesitated, then said: 'All right. To begin with, it was just an affair. Nothing serious, just a bit of fun, a bit of excitement. I assumed that when Claude moved away, out of Paris, that would be the end of it; things would go back to the way they were before. But they didn't. The whole thing made me look at Philippe in a new light, and I didn't much like what I saw.

'He was always rather gauche, sentimental – all red roses and love letters. Like, for example, he kept a scrap-book full of photographs and notes about places we'd been to together; he sort of sanctified them, made shrines out of them. He had a calendar, too, of silly anniversaries – the first time we slept together, the first time we went to the Louvre together, the day we had dinner at the Tour d'Argent, that sort of nonsense. He even used to put little lovey-dovey messages in the newspaper, sometimes, in the Personal column, to commemorate these momentous occasions.'

How interesting, thought Andrieu.

'At first,' she said, 'it was quite charming; flattering. I suppose that's why I married him. But after a while, it began to feel cloying, oppressive – like drowning in syrup. And he wasn't even much good in bed. Compared with Claude, he was a fumbling schoolboy. I could put up with it so long as Claude was still around, but once he'd gone, and there was just Philippe . . . ugh, I couldn't stand it; I just couldn't bear to have him touch me. He didn't understand why, and I couldn't explain.

'He kept on and on at me, trying to find out what was the matter. He fussed over me all the time, thought I was ill, tried to get me to go to the doctor. He was driving me crazy. Then one day he came home with a big stupid grin on his face and a pair of tickets for a Caribbean cruise. A second honeymoon, he said.

'I couldn't bear it. The thought of being trapped with him on a ship for two weeks – I'd have jumped overboard. I blew my top. I just screamed and yelled at him; I told him he repulsed me.'

'And that's when you told him about Claude?' Andrieu said.

'I didn't intend to; it just came out.'

'How did he react?'

'Predictably. First, he got mad; then he burst into tears. It went on like that for weeks. When I couldn't stand it any longer, I moved out. I wouldn't tell him where I was going, because I knew he'd never leave me alone, but he found out anyway and kept on pestering me. So I got myself a lawyer and started divorce proceedings; and then the chance of a job in Bordeaux came up, and I jumped at it. Anything to get away from him.'

She was on her third cigarette by now.

Andrieu said, 'Did he ever make any threats against Claude?'

'Oh, all the time. He was going to kill him, make him suffer, ruin his life – give him a taste of his own medicine and see how he liked it. He told me he'd found out where Claude was living, where he was working, what he was doing; he said he wasn't going to let him get away with it.'

'Did you believe he really meant it? Would he have been capable of carrying out his threats?'

'I honestly don't know. He wasn't particularly hard or tough – but he could get very emotional, and then he seemed to lose control. He hit me a few times, towards the end . . .'

'Did you have any contact with him after the divorce?'

'He kept trying to get in touch with me. He'd write to me at the office, but I'd tear up the letters without reading them; and he'd phone and try to talk to me, but they'd say I wasn't in. This went on for years. And then suddenly – about eighteen months ago, I think it was – it stopped. I don't know why. I did hear that he was in therapy; maybe it worked. Maybe he finally grew up and got a grip on reality.'

'You know he got married again?'

'No, I didn't.' She was surprised, a little curious; probably would have liked to know more, but felt it beneath her dignity to ask. 'But then,' she said, dismissively, 'I wouldn't have expected to know. As you can imagine, I haven't made any attempt to keep in touch or find out what he's doing.'

'What about you – when did you remarry?'

'About four years ago. Charles is in the wine trade, too; that's how we met.'

'Are you happy?'

'I think that's a rather impertinent question. Are you?' She blew a stream of smoke at him. 'Look, before we go any further, I'd like to know what's going on here. Why do you want to know all this?'

'In a moment,' he said firmly. 'Just a few more questions first. Do you ever regret the break-up of your first marriage? Do you think it might have survived if it hadn't been for Claude?'

'No, and no again. That's what I kept trying to tell Philippe – the problem wasn't Claude, it was him. He was smothering me. But he wouldn't listen.'

'And Claude – how do you feel about him, after all these years?'

'That's another impertinent question.'

'All the same, I'd appreciate an answer.'

'I don't feel anything in particular. I hardly think about him at all. It was a long time ago.'

'You don't hold him responsible for what happened?'

'Like I said: it would have happened anyway.'

'Or feel resentful because he broke off the affair?'

'He didn't break it off; it just became impractical, once he'd left Paris. And I knew all along that that was going to happen. The move was arranged before we even started the affair. Now, are you going to tell me what's going on?'

He said, cautiously: 'Claude Chavanac had a serious car crash earlier this summer. You may have read about it in the newspapers.'

Her eyebrows rose above the plume of cigarette smoke, in an expression of apparently genuine surprise.

'No. When was this?'

'In June.'

'Ah, that explains it. Charles and I spent most of June in California, touring the Napa Valley vineyards. We didn't get to hear much news from home.'

'Yes, I see. I suppose you could prove that, could you?'

'That we were in California? Yes, of course we could – but I can't imagine why we should have to. What are you suggesting? That this car crash wasn't an accident, is that what you're saying?'

'It's a possibility we're investigating. Tell me, did Philippe know much about cars?'

Her mouth curled around a stream of smoke.

'Is the Pope Catholic?' she said, and crossed her legs again.

All right, so it was strictly against orders. He should have been on his way back up the *autoroute,* not still here in Gordes, lingering over a coffee and a sandwich in a tourist bar full of international culture junkies. His brief was to interview Francine Julien and that was all. He was not, under any circumstances, to approach Philippe Rocard. Rocard must not know he was under suspicion until they had a watertight case against him.

But, come on, how watertight can you get?

Consider: a man – a romantic and not very mature man – falls obsessively in love with a glamorous woman. He showers her with presents and inducements, and finally persuades her to marry him. He lives with her in blissful contentment for a number of years; and if she's not as besotted as he is, she doesn't let it show. Then she suddenly turns moody, won't let him touch her, and finally admits she's been having an affair, and that now she finds him repulsive.

The marriage collapses in ruins. He's desolate. He convinces himself that his wife's lover has turned her against him; he can't bring himself to blame the woman he loves, so he puts all the blame on the man. He won't let go. The thing festers for years. He keeps trying to contact his wife. Then he gives up. Why?

Could it be because he's switched on to a new tack? Change of tactics. Change of target.

He's kept tabs on his wife's lover; he knows where he lives, what he does. The media will have helped: he'll have seen all the publicity surrounding the murder case the lover was involved in last year. Maybe that's what triggers him into action. He's threatened to get his own back on this man; now he's going to do it. It takes time, a lot of planning. The lover lives in a remote part of the country. He has to wait for – or create – an opportunity to go there.

He does well in his job; he gets promoted to sales manager. He draws up a sales plan that targets the very area where his wife's lover now lives. A perfect excuse to be there. And when he gets there, he begins to persecute this man with a series of nasty and dangerous little incidents . . .

Of course, there is one other possibility.

It just might be that the wife harbours a grudge against her lover. He's gone off and left her dissatisfied with her husband; he's destroyed her marriage. Suppose she's been brooding about it all these years, and finally decided to take action? After all, she's spending her summer vacation in Gordes, less than half an hour's drive from where her lover is staying.

Unfortunately for this fine theory, she was in California when several of these incidents occurred. She says she can prove it, and she probably can. Why claim an alibi like that if you can't prove it?

And anyway, what does she know about cars? Whereas her ex-husband's an expert: according to her, he loves tinkering with engines; does a bit of rally driving, too. It checks out – a phone call to an old friend who happens to be a sports journalist; quick scan through the sports database, and there's the husband's name showing up in a couple of big rally-driving events. Just the sort of man who'd know how to fix the brakes on the lover's car to make it crash.

Does he mean to kill the lover, or just scare the shit out of him? Who knows? The lover survives. So the husband tries a few other things. And then, when the lover goes on holiday, he follows him. He must be pretty obsessed, to do that. But then we already know, from the way he behaved towards his wife, he's an obsessive personality.

We know, too, that he has a penchant for putting small ads in newspapers. And that he works with computers – which means he'd have no difficulty in producing word-processed, laser-printed letters. He might even have a portable computer with him here in Provence – Andrieu remembers a salesman who wheedled his way into police HQ one time, and he had a neat little number, with a flip-up screen and its own built-in printer, that he carried around with him all the time. With something like that, Rocard could print his letters to the newspapers even in some remote little village, without access to an office.

We know all this. How much more do we need?

If it walks like a duck and *coins* like a duck, it's a duck.

Albuisson replaced the telephone handset on its cradle with a deep and mournful sigh. Why can't life be just a little more straightforward? he thought.

The list of suspects for the Chavanac business was like a moving staircase; every time he looked, there was a different name at the top. First it was Brunet, and that seemed pretty definite; the man practically incriminated himself. But then it seemed that he couldn't have done it after all; not in the right place at the right time.

So, next, Philippe Rocard rises to the surface. Motive, opportunity, and lots of circumstantial evidence: practically home and dry.

Then comes a phone call from Zoe Chavanac.

The Hippopotamus has disappeared. Nobody knows why, or where she's gone. But it happened right after the midget saw Albuisson nosing around their Mercedes, and drove off as though the hounds of hell were after him. Coincidence, or what?

Zoe has tried to find out where they've gone. She's let it be known around the village that when the Hippopotamus last visited the Chavanacs' villa, she accidentally left behind an expensive silk shawl; Zoe had intended to return it the next time they met, but now, as it seems there'll be no next time, she's anxious to send it on to her by post. But she doesn't know the woman's address in Paris, and she wonders if anyone else might have it?

The villagers, Zoe says, have been most helpful. Several have come forward with the address the woman gave them – the caretaker of the villa she'd been renting, the local shopkeeper with whom she had an account, and several others who'd been given the Paris address for one reason or another.

And every address is different.

16

Andrieu took a quick look around the village. That was all it took – one glance, and you'd seen all there was to see. He couldn't imagine why people travelled miles to spend their holidays in places like this. In the heat of the afternoon, the only sign of life was a busybody mongrel urgently trotting back and forth across the square; an older, wiser dog lay snoring in the shade of the fountain.

Andrieu spotted the bar, and went in. It was cooler inside, but not much. A lazy fan, suspended from the ceiling, stirred the heat around; flies buzzed aimlessly. Two men, in singlets and shorts, stood at the counter, drinking beer. Andrieu joined them, and ordered a beer for himself. He asked the barman if he happened to know where Philippe Rocard and his wife were staying.

The barman was cagey. 'You a mate of his, then?'

'Colleague,' said Andrieu, inventively. 'Computer business.'

'Computers,' echoed one of the drinkers. 'That's the thing.'

'What thing?' said his friend.

'The future. That's what it's all about. Computers.'

'Yeah,' said the friend. They both sighed and stared into their beer.

'I was in Avignon, doing a bit of business,' Andrieu said to the barman. 'Didn't take as long as I expected, so I had some time to kill, and I knew Philippe was staying round here somewhere so I thought I might stop by, say hello.'

'Is he the one with the wife?' said the first drinker.

'What, that one?' said the second, cupping his hands some considerable distance from his chest.

'Yes, that one.'

'Yes, he is,' said the barman.

This could be interesting, thought Andrieu. 'So you do know them?' he said to the barman.

'Yes, they come in here. They're staying in a villa up the top of the village – big green gates; can't miss it.'

'Cheers,' said Andrieu.

The big green gates stood open. Andrieu strolled through them and along a short driveway towards the house. There was a car parked outside; he gave it a casual inspection: sports engine, four-wheel drive, wide wheels and go-faster stripes. Interesting.

He followed a narrow, paved path around the perimeter of the house, until he came to a hedge of young cypresses. Through the branches there were sparks of blue: swimming pool. He skirted the hedge and arrived at an iron gate, and beyond that he could see the pool. There was someone swimming – a woman in a wide-brimmed hat, performing a perfunctory breast stroke with her head held erect above the water.

As Andrieu watched, she swam to the end of the pool and began to climb out. She reached the top of the steps, and slid her feet into a pair of sandals lying by the poolside. In between the hat and the sandals, she was wearing nothing else at all. His eyebrows rose, and more besides. This was Rocard's wife? The man in the bar had not exaggerated; if anything, he had rather understated the case.

She turned and saw him. 'Oh, hello,' she said – surprised, but not in the least embarrassed. 'Can I help you?'

'Um,' said Andrieu, lost for words. 'Um . . . I was looking for Philippe Rocard.'

'Oh, that's my husband,' she said. 'He's inside. Too hot for him, out here. Me, I love it.'

She was, he could hardly help noticing, golden brown and glistening all over.

'Mind you,' she said, 'you do have to be careful. These warnings you hear – radiation damage and ozone and all that. But if you listened to everything they say, you'd never do anything, would you? Anyway, I use a good sunscreen. And I always wear a hat.'

Andrieu nodded. 'That's all right, then. Um, your husband . . .?'

'Just go in,' she said. She gestured nonchalantly towards the house, scattering a shower of water droplets and making everything wobble.

He gulped. 'Yes. Right,' he said.

Inside the house, the light was dim and the air was relatively cool. There was a large room, pleasantly furnished, with several doors leading off. Andrieu glanced around, noting details: a vase of bright flowers on a sideboard, an untidy pile of magazines – and, on a small table in the corner, a portable computer. Yes! he thought, with satisfaction.

The house was silent. Andrieu called out: 'Hello?'

Sounds of movement, then a man appeared at one of the doors. Andrieu looked him over: tall, average-looking, balding, chunky moustache; baggy T-shirt, shapeless shorts and thin, hairy legs with ludicrous lumpy knees. He thought of Francine Julien crossing her elegant legs – not to mention the voluptuous vision outside. How did a nerd like this pull women like that?

'Are you Philippe Rocard?' he said.

The man nodded. 'And you?' He spoke pleasantly – neither aggressive nor defensive; not even particularly surprised to find a stranger in his living-room.

Andrieu showed his ID and rattled off his credentials. 'I'm investigating a series of incidents involving a man named Claude Chavanac,' he said. 'I believe you know him.'

'Oh, yes.' Disappointingly, Rocard seemed not in the least disconcerted. 'He and his family are staying at a villa not far from here,' he said. 'Quite a coincidence, actually – we used to be neighbours in Paris, years ago.'

Andrieu said, provocatively: 'He was a bit more than just a neighbour, surely.'

'I'm not sure what you mean.'

'Well, he was your wife's lover, wasn't he? Your first wife, I mean.'

Rocard sighed. 'Oh, now I see what this is all about. Someone's been having a go at him, have they? And you think it's me.'

'I understand,' said Andrieu, 'that at one time you made certain threats against him.'

'In the heat of the moment, yes. Wouldn't you?'

'I don't know. I've never found myself in that situation. But your wife – I mean, your ex-wife – she gave me the impression that this wasn't merely in the heat of the moment. It went on for several years.'

'Oh, you've been talking to Francine, have you? You're privileged. She's very particular about who she talks to.' Rocard paused for thought. 'Let me tell you how it was. I was really screwed up for a while. I suppose I did sound off against Chavanac, but most of it was hot air. I had to get mad at someone. And if the chance had arisen, if I'd met him in the street – well, yes, I suppose I might have done something. But he was out in the provinces somewhere, and I was in Paris, so I wasn't going to run into him by accident – and I didn't have the willpower to make it happen. I was too busy feeling sorry for myself.

'I used to dream up schemes in my head, what I'd like to do to him if I got the chance – but if ever I had got the chance, I suspect, I'd have ducked it. Trying to live out your fantasies is a mistake, I always find. It never turns out like you expect. Best to stick with the fantasy.'

'Do you still have these . . . fantasies?'

'No. I'm glad to say I grew out of it. You know how? I'd tried everything: counselling, psychotherapy, pills, new-age mystical rubbish – complete waste of time. Then I went out and got drunk one night, with an old friend, and it all got very maudlin, the way these things do. I was drivelling on about how wonderful Francine was, as usual, and he suddenly announced that he'd always thought she was an absolute bitch, and never understood why I married her in the first place.

'I got mad as hell for a moment, nearly hit him; and then I thought, sod it, he's right. *In vino veritas*. Another fantasy, you see; I had this image of what she was like, the perfect woman – and she wasn't like that at all, but I just couldn't see it. Not until that moment. I woke up next morning with the happiest hangover in the world, and that's when I started to clear out my head. It was like clearing out an old cupboard full of junk.

'I did try to contact Francine, tell her she could relax, it was all over – but, as usual, she wouldn't talk to me, so she never found out. I don't suppose she even knew I'd got married again?'

'No, she didn't. When did that happen?'

'About eighteen months ago, though I'd known Joelle for a while before that. She worked for the same company as me, on the switchboard. She was good fun; we used to joke together a lot, go for a drink after work, that sort of thing. But when I still had my head full of Francine, I never thought of other women as – well, as women, you know? I'd convinced myself that there'd never be anyone else for me. Then I saw the light – and I saw Jo-Jo, and I thought to myself: Rocard, what is the matter with you? This girl is gorgeous, she's fun – and she doesn't behave like she's a goddess. Oh, I know there are those who think she's just a silly little bimbo; and she's certainly no intellectual – thank God. But she's got no airs and graces; she accepts people for what they are. She's open and she's honest – what you see is what you get.'

And you get to see most of it, thought Andrieu.

'She's done wonders for me,' Rocard said. 'The thing with Francine completely destroyed my self-respect. My career was going down the tubes; I went into the office every day expecting to be fired. With Jo-Jo, it's all different. I started getting bonuses, promotions.

'Of course, it wasn't all plain sailing. It wasn't easy to unhitch from Francine; there were a lot of ghosts to lay. That's why we're here – she and I had some good times in this area, back in the old days. I had to force myself to face up to all those memories. I thought it was going to be difficult – but in fact it hasn't been difficult at all. As for Claude Chavanac, the first time I came face-to-face with him, I felt like shaking him by the hand and thanking him. If it hadn't been for him, I'd probably still have been stuck with that toffee-nosed bitch.'

'I take it you didn't actually do that, though?'

'Well, no. There were rather a lot of people around, including his wife; it might have been a little awkward to explain.'

Andrieu had his notebook out of his pocket.

'I wonder', he said, 'if by any chance you could tell me where you were on these dates: Thursday the 9th of June, Tuesday the 28th June, and Friday the 8th of July.'

He expected the usual response: How the hell am I supposed to remember? Can you remember what you were doing on some random date two months ago? But Rocard said, quite calmly: 'No, not off the top of my head. It'll be in the computer, though.'

He marched across to the corner table, switched on the computer and opened it up. It whirred and buzzed a bit, and on the screen appeared the image of a diary.

'It's all in here,' he said. 'Appointments, addresses, phone numbers, account numbers, the works. Have you got one of these?'

Andrieu shook his head.

'You should. Worth its weight in gold, I promise you.'

Once a salesman, always a salesman, thought Andrieu. I've as good as accused him of a serious criminal offence, and here he is, trying to sell me a bloody computer.

Rocard said: 'What were those dates? Thursday the 9th of June, did you say? Oh yes, we were in Clermont-Ferrand all that week.'

Clermont-Ferrand: it wouldn't take long to get from there to St-Flour, not these days, since they opened the new *autoroute*.

Andrieu said: 'Who's "we"?'

'Me and my regional sales team. Four of us, selling computers.' Rocard tapped the screen, itemising the details. 'You see, there: on the Thursday, we were running demonstrations at the Chamber of Commerce. Not one of our better days; a few reasonable leads, but we only closed a couple of sales.'

'You were there all day?'

'Yes.'

'Did you break for lunch?'

'I can't say I remember, but I shouldn't think so. On these sales trips, unless I'm having lunch with a client, I prefer to grab a sandwich and work right through, and then relax over a decent meal in the evening.'

'Would there have been someone with you all the time that day?'

'Well, I didn't take anyone with me when I went for a piss, but apart from that . . .'

'What about the next date, the 28th of June?'

More information flashed up on the screen.

'We were in St-Geraud that week. Same kind of thing: sales visits, demos, exhibitions. And the 8th of July, by then we'd moved on to Le Puy. That was the last week of the roadshow – running into the holiday period; the pickings were getting pretty thin by then.'

'Can we just go back to the St-Geraud visit, for a moment? What were you doing on the Tuesday?'

Rocard peered at the screen. 'Special promotion at a computer shop.' He sounded vague.

'You don't seem to remember it very clearly.'

'On these trips, one computer shop is very much like another.'

There was the sound of approaching footsteps, and Joelle Rocard's voice from behind them: 'What are you two up to?'

Andrieu hardly dared to turn around. When he did, he saw that she had taken off her hat and wrapped herself – but only just – in a towelling robe. He couldn't decide if this made matters better or worse. Every time she moved, the loosely tied robe threatened to fall open, creating an air of uncertainty that made it rather difficult to concentrate. At least, before, you knew where you were.

Her husband said: 'We're trying to figure out what I was doing on the 28th of June.'

'The 28th of June?' she said, wrinkling her forehead in thought. 'Oh, that was – you know . . .'

'No, I don't.'

'Course you do.'

She went to the pile of magazines on the table; they were all about health and beauty or computers. She pulled one out, flicked it open and thrust it in front of Andrieu.

'Of course!' said Rocard. 'The sales awards. That's why I don't remember being in St-Geraud that day. I wasn't there. I took a couple of days out – left on the Monday night, back on Wednesday.'

'He was European Sales Manager of the Year,' said Joelle, proudly. 'It was great! There was this big awards ceremony – in *London*. They flew us over there, put us up at the Dorchester Hotel, we had this big formal dinner and everything . . .'

And there she was to prove it, in the picture in the magazine:

big smile, big hair, spectacular cleavage; and there was Philippe Rocard beside her, clutching her in one hand and some kind of award in the other.

Andrieu turned to the front cover. It was the house magazine for the American company that Rocard worked for. The text was in English, not French, but the photo caption was easy enough to understand. It said: 'Philippe Rocard, European Sales Manager of the Year, with his wife Joelle, after receiving his award from Sales Vice-President Andrew Rockwell, at the European Managers' Convention in London's Dorchester Hotel.'

And the date of this event was pretty clear in either language: Tuesday, 28th June.

17

'You should have heard him,' Andrieu said, 'blustering away – he couldn't decide if he should tear me off a strip for disregarding orders, or give me a commendation for using my initiative.'

He had phoned Albuisson from Provence, to give him the news of Philippe Rocard's alibi, and then driven straight back to St-Geraud, dictating his report of the day's events into his portable tape recorder as he drove along. He had stopped off at HQ to dump the tapes and check for messages; on his desk, he'd found a note from Albuisson and a set of photographs developed from the rolls of film Albuisson had brought back from Provence.

He flicked through them briefly and stuck them in his pocket to study more carefully some other time. It was very late by now, and he was tired, too tired to concentrate – but still on a high, not ready to sleep yet. So he'd dropped into a bar where you could get a drink just about any time, and there he'd found an old friend, Matthieu. Matthieu was police, too. Most of the after-hours drinkers were police. One time, this bar had been raided by the drug squad, after a – presumably ironic – tip-off; they hadn't found a single civilian in the place.

Now Andrieu was telling his story to Matthieu.

'This Rocard is odd,' he said. 'Wears his heart on his sleeve. He'll tell you anything. He just talked and talked – I hardly had to ask a single question. I had to believe him, even before we got to the alibi. This was one happy man – and if you'd seen that wife of his, you'd know why.'

'Was she really, you know, completely . . .'

'. . . stark bollock-naked,' said Andrieu, somewhat inappropriately. 'Well, apart from the hat.'

He reached into his pocket and pulled out one of the snapshots he'd found on his desk.

'That's her.'

The photograph showed Joelle Rocard in the foreground, leaning forward in the act of pitching a *boule*. She was clothed, but not excessively.

Matthieu whistled softly. 'Some people get all the interesting jobs.'

Andrieu shrugged. 'Some you win, some you lose.' He showed Matthieu another photograph. '*This* is the next assignment.'

'Christ, what the hell is that?'

'A woman called de Sousa. We think she's in Paris, but she's left a trail of false addresses. Albuisson wants me to track her down. I've got a few contacts in the Paris police – Didier Roc, remember him, he's working up there now? – and some others you wouldn't know. I'll get on to them in the morning, and hope they come up with the goods.'

Matthieu was transfixed by the photograph.

'Imagine coming across *that* with no clothes on,' he said.

Friday morning, half-past six, Hugo rolled over and grunted.

'What's that sound?' he mumbled.

Moira said, sleepily: 'Sounds like it's coming from Zoe and Claude's room.'

Hugo considered. 'Claude's leg must be getting better,' he said.

'Well, it is their wedding anniversary,' said Moira.

*

Albuisson sat sifting papers, getting nowhere. The image of the moving staircase had faded; now he saw a row of tin ducks on a fairground shooting gallery, gliding along smugly, one by one.

Brunet: out of range.

Rocard: shielded by an unchallengeable alibi for June 28th, the night of the fire at the Chavanacs' house – and, although they hadn't checked it out yet, it seemed a safe bet that there'd be independent witnesses to place him firmly in Clermont-Ferrand right through the day of the car crash.

And now the Hippopotamus: the biggest target of all, but seemingly impossible to hit.

Time was passing by; it was the 19th of August already. He wanted to get to the bottom of this case while the Chavanacs and their tormentor were still in Provence, but here he was with the *rentrée* less than two weeks away, and no closer to any kind of conclusion.

The priority now must be to find the de Sousa woman – but so far they were getting nowhere. Andrieu's enquiries, through his contacts in the Paris police, had so far been fruitless. And there was always the risk that this, like the pursuit of Rocard, might turn out to be just another false trail. Much as he preferred to do one thing at a time, he couldn't afford to keep other lines of enquiry on hold until they found her.

He turned to the notes on the Grissot trial. Andrieu had tracked down a copy of the original court reports, and a batch of ten-year-old newspaper cuttings, but they added little to the information Chavanac had already given him. He'd been unable to turn up a telephone number for either of Chavanac's two guilty clients, Jean-Michel Artaud and Richard Dullin; enquiries at past addresses had drawn a blank.

There was, though, a number, which Andrieu had got from Chavanac's secretary, for Laurent Jouvet, the client who'd been acquitted. But when Albuisson had dialled it earlier in the day, all he got was Jouvet's answering machine. Well, at least it confirmed that Jouvet was still at that number. But not at home; probably on holiday, like everyone else. All that Albuisson could do was to leave his name and number and hope for the best.

Frustrated now, he strolled out of his office and across to

Andrieu's desk, pondering and tapping his teeth with a pencil. Andrieu was out somewhere; on the pinboard by his desk, he had stuck up a selection of the Chavanacs' photographs. Albuisson noticed with mild disapproval that the ones he had chosen seemed to feature Joelle Rocard rather prominently, in several respects (Andrieu had not seen fit to disclose to him the details of his encounter by the Rocards' swimming pool, but he had reckoned without the power of the grapevine, the only system in the building that still functioned efficiently even in August).

Albuisson scanned the other faces in the photographs: the de Sousa woman, the pair they called the Newlyweds, the elderly couple, the villagers, the foreigners . . . who, who, who? In the background, he heard a telephone ringing.

Gradually, he realized it must be his own extension. No one answered it; secretarial support was thin on the ground. He hurried back to his desk.

'Hello, yes?'

The switchboard operator said: 'Call from Paris for you, a M. Laurent Jouvet? Says you left a message on his answerphone.'

'I'll take it,' said Albuisson.

By way of an anniversary celebration, Claude was taking Zoe for dinner at a rather fine restaurant in a village some distance away. Neither of them planned to be in a fit state to drive home, so it was arranged that Hugo would drive them there; they would come back by taxi.

The restaurant was perched at the top of the village, and the village was perched at the top of a hill. Big windows surveyed a panoramic sunset. Inside, there was starched linen, plain crystal and good silverware. Champagne was brought; Zoe cast an eye over the menu.

'Mmm, nice,' she said. 'Georges would love this.'

'The hell with Georges,' said Claude. 'I don't want to think about him, or anything else to do with this . . . business. Not tonight.' He scanned the room. 'Oh, look, here come your English friends.'

Zoe turned, to see the *maître d'* welcoming the two young men from Suffolk.

'I'm not sure how friendly they are, after Hugo was rude to them.'

'Hugo's rude to everyone.'

The pair apparently bore no grudge. They stopped as they went by on the way to their table.

'Hello. Fancy seeing you here,' said the taller one.

'Small world,' said the other.

'Celebrating?' said the tall one, noticing the champagne.

'It's our anniversary,' said Zoe.

'Well, there's a coincidence,' said the shorter one, smiling benignly at his companion. 'Ours too.'

Claude raised his glass. 'Congratulations,' he said.

'Have a nice meal,' said the tall one.

They did. And as they were leaving, stopping in the lobby to ask the *maître d'* to summon the village taxi, the young men came by on their way out.

'We're going in your direction,' the taller one said. 'We can give you a lift if you like.'

'You'll be quite safe,' said the shorter one. 'He doesn't drink.' He beamed beatifically. 'All the more for me.'

'That's very kind of you,' said Zoe.

'You all wait here,' said the taller one, mindful of Claude's locomotive problems. 'I'll bring the car round.'

Minutes later, he was back, tight-lipped.

'Come and look at this,' he said.

They all stepped outside. There was a light blue Volvo parked in the narrow street in front of the restaurant. Light blue except for the great ugly splash of red paint over the bonnet, and the word 'salaud' sprayed along the side.

'You're going to Paris on *Sunday*?' Madame Albuisson said, incredulously. Georges never went anywhere on Sundays if he could help it, except in the interests of lunch.

'There's no alternative. I need to see this man Jouvet. He's been working away from home all this week – he phoned me as soon as he got back; and he's off to Germany for a fortnight on Monday, so Sunday's the only day I can see him.'

'Couldn't you just have talked to him on the phone?'

'I'd rather see him in person. You can learn a lot more that way.'

'But why do you have to go? Why not send young Andrieu? He wouldn't mind.'

'I'm sure he wouldn't. But he's like a bull in a china shop.'

All right, so the Rocard business had turned out for the best, and they'd saved a lot of time; if Andrieu hadn't gone in there, against orders, they might still have been chasing down that particular dead end. But he could easily have come unstuck. Albuisson wasn't prepared to let him loose on Paris.

'I'd prefer to do this myself,' he said.

'Well,' his wife sniffed, 'if you must.'

In Provence, there were clouds. Not the usual dinky little fine-weather clouds, put there just to show off the blue of the sky. These were big, grey, serious clouds, loitering on the horizon like troops awaiting orders to invade.

'I suppose it makes a nice change for the weather forecasters,' said Hugo.

The air was hot and clinging; it wrapped itself around you like a boa constrictor. The water in the swimming pools felt thick and moved like mercury. People slowly ground to a halt, as though their batteries were running down, and even the crickets were silenced. In the village square, Chiara took all her clothes off and sat in the fountain. Everyone applauded, declared it the most sensible thing they'd seen all day, and why didn't they all do it? But, of course, no one did; not even Joelle.

Paris, too, was stifling. Laurent Jouvet's directions led Albuisson to a brutally modern apartment building, all concrete and metal and dark grey linoleum. But the brutally modern lift wore an old-fashioned 'out of order' notice; he puffed his way up the stairs to Jouvet's fourth-floor flat.

Jouvet was a lean, good-looking man, forty-something, in jeans and a casual shirt, and a pair of expensively fashionable boots. He ushered his visitor into a large, sparsely furnished and mercifully air-conditioned room, with blond wood floors and black venetian blinds. Elevated beyond the noise of the street, and with the double-glazed windows firmly closed, it was uncannily cool and quiet.

Invited to take a seat, Albuisson perched on a chair of the kind that he had always assumed went directly from designer to museum, without any intervening period of domesticity; it had never occurred to him that anyone would use them for sitting on. It was exquisitely uncomfortable, and probably worth a fortune; he was terrified that it might collapse under his weight.

Jouvet left the room and returned with a bottle of chilled Badoit and two elegant glasses. The echoing silence was broken only by the gentle fizzing of the water.

'Thank you for making the time to see me,' said Albuisson. 'You seem to be a very busy man.'

'Well, I travel about a lot.'

'What exactly do you do?'

'I'm a journalist – legal correspondent. I used to practise law, but it's a bore, an old man's job. This is much more fun.' He handed Albuisson a cold glass. 'Now, what can I do for you? You mentioned on the phone that it was something to do with the Grissot case. That's going back a long way, you know. I'm not sure I can remember an awful lot about it; to be honest, it's the kind of thing one's only too glad to forget.'

'I appreciate that. But it's not so much the details of the case that concern me. I'm trying to trace two of your co-defendents, Richard Dullin and Jean-Michel Artaud, and I wondered if you'd know where they are now, or if you could tell me anything about them.'

Jouvet took a long drink of water. 'Well, I'm not sure,' he said. 'Richard underwent some sort of religious conversion – the full road-to-Damascus number, so I heard. When he came out of gaol, he couldn't cope with the real world. He didn't have any support, I suppose that was the problem: no job to go back to, no family – he wasn't married and in all the years I knew him I never heard him mention any relatives. Jesus was probably all he had.'

'Did you see him at all, after he came out?'

'Oh, yes, we met up a couple of times. But we didn't have a lot to say to each other; he was on another wavelength. In the end, he went off to be a monk, or a hermit, or something. He joined some obscure religious community – near Grenoble, I think it was. As far as I know he's still there. I can probably dig up the name of the place, if you want, though I don't know whether you'd get to speak to him. I understand it's one of those enclosed, silent orders – they cut themselves off from the world to contemplate God and keep bees, that sort of thing.'

'I see,' said Albuisson, beginning to feel depressed. 'Well, what about the other man, Artaud?'

'No idea, sorry. Haven't seen him for years. My wife might be able to help you, though. She was quite friendly with Marie-Christine at one time – that's his wife; I mean, she used to be. They're divorced now. They had two boys about the same age as our kids – same schools, same friends, so our wives used to see quite a lot of one another. I don't know whether they're still in touch, but it's possible.'

'In that case, I'd like to talk to your wife. What time will she be home?'

Jouvet grimaced. 'You'll have a long wait. Danielle doesn't live here; we split up about eight months ago.'

'Ah. Sorry. Didn't realize.'

'No reason why you should. No particular reason to be sorry, either. It wasn't a painful separation. It was just a long-term state of affairs reaching its logical conclusion. Up here,' – he tapped his head – 'we'd been separated for years.'

'Did that have anything to do with the Grissot case?'

'Good lord, no. That was – well, I suppose it was traumatic at the time, but we were always confident that I'd be acquitted. And afterwards, things went back to normal pretty quickly. I don't think it had any lasting effect on my career – if anything, I gained from the sympathy factor. People felt I'd been badly done to. No, something much worse happened not long afterwards – we lost a child, our youngest. It was an accident, no one was to blame; but things were never the same after that. Do you have children?'

Albuisson shook his head. He and his wife had never made any conscious decision on the matter: if it had happened, he would have accepted it willingly, but it hadn't, and he had never felt greatly deprived. He found it hard to imagine how it felt to be a parent.

Jouvet said: 'We carried on for the sake of the other two kids, but once they were out on their own – our youngest started university last year – there didn't seem much point in staying together.'

'You have your wife's address, I suppose.'

'Yes, of course. I'll write it down for you. And I'll see if I can find the name of that monastery, or whatever it is.'

Albuisson cautiously rose from his chair. 'While you're doing that, perhaps I might use your WC?'

'Of course. Over there, the third door.'

The bathroom was in keeping with the rest of the apartment: black, white and stainless steel, and a cantilevered toilet with no visible means of support. The usual bathroom detritus, if it existed, was hidden away behind mirrored cupboard doors, except for one pristine white hand-towel, a bar of disconcertingly black soap, and – no doubt by accident rather than design – on the floor behind the bidet, a pair of very brief, pink knickers.

18

Albuisson sweltered in the back of a taxi as it crawled round the *périphérique*; if this was Sunday afternoon in an empty August Paris, he hoped he'd never find himself here in a wet winter rush-hour.

Danielle Jouvet lived in a middle-class suburb, fourteen floors up. The block was less self-consciously stylish than her husband's, but at least the lifts were working. Albuisson had called ahead from Laurent Jouvet's apartment, so she was expecting him. She was a small, rather pretty, dark-haired woman with a sad smile.

'Do come in,' she said. 'Isn't it hot? Would you like some lemonade? It's home-made.'

Her apartment was as cluttered and chintzy as her husband's was pared-down and chic. Albuisson sank into a flowery sofa, and sipped his lemonade. It was uncommonly good.

He said: 'As I explained on the phone, I'm trying to trace

Jean-Michel Artaud. Your husband said you used to be friendly with his ex-wife, and he thought you might still be in touch with her.'

'Marie-Christine? Yes, we kept in contact for a number of years. I spent a lot of time with her after Jean-Mich first went to prison. She took it very badly, didn't want anything more to do with him. We all tried to persuade her to wait – it wasn't so very long, he only got eighteen months, and I thought she ought to give him another chance, if only for the sake of the boys. But she said it was for their sake she was doing it; she didn't want them growing up under the influence of a criminal. She was very unforgiving.'

'So what did she do?'

'She went home to her parents. They had a farm; sheep, I think. She used to write to me quite often. She divorced Jean-Mich and went back to using her maiden name. Eventually, she met another man – he was a teacher at the school the boys went to – and they got married and moved to Brittany; that's where he came from. She wrote once more after that, but then the letters stopped. I kept on writing for a while, but she never replied, so I gave up in the end. I would have liked to keep in touch, but I can understand why she might not. She's got a new life now; I expect I'm part of the past that she wants to forget.'

'But as far as you know she's still at the same address in Brittany?'

'I think so.'

'What about her ex-husband? Have you had any contact with him? Do you know where he is?'

'I haven't seen him since the trial. I do know that after he came out of prison – he couldn't go back to his legal career, for obvious reasons – he got a job with a company that published legal textbooks, based in Lille, I think. But later on, Marie-Christine said he'd moved back to Paris.'

'So she did still have some contact with him. Do you think she'd know where he is now?'

'Oh, I'm sure she would. She may not have wanted anything to do with him, but he is the boys' father, and there were occasions when he had to be involved – you know, signatures on official documents, things like that. So she always made a point of knowing how to get hold of him if she had to. I'll get you her address, shall I? I don't think I've got her phone number, I'm afraid.'

She rummaged in a jumbled dresser drawer. Albuisson stood up and wandered to the window. Paris sprawled below in the hot hazy distance.

'Quite a view,' he said.

There were photographs ranged along the windowsill. A chubby toddler: the child that had died? A boy and a girl at various ages, growing from cheerful children to sulky teenagers, the boy scowling and the girl peering out, barely visible, between curtains of long dark hair. Here they were on their own, and there with their mother, with other people – but never with their father. Had Danielle Jouvet edited him out of her life? Or was it simply that he had always been the family photographer?

'Ah, here it is,' she said, pulling out a tattered address book. She copied an address on to a scrap of paper and handed it to Albuisson. He squinted to read her writing.

'Marie-Christine Brasseur?'

'That's her new name, since she remarried.'

The address was in Rennes. In the cab back to the city centre, Albuisson pondered. The more he heard about this woman, the more he began to wonder whether she might not be as likely a suspect as her ex-husband. It sounded as though the Grissot affair had had a disastrous effect on her life; and, from the way the Jouvets spoke of her, it would appear that she had a vindictive streak. She had blamed her husband for her misfortunes; might she also have blamed his lawyer?

She certainly merited further investigation. But how? Should he phone the Rennes police, get them to question her? Or would it be better to do it himself? Find her phone number and call her? Or go there in person? If he turned up unannounced, she wouldn't be prepared for him, wouldn't have the chance to conceal anything that she might want to hide. That could be useful. On the other hand, she might be on vacation, and his journey would be wasted. On balance, though, it was probably a chance worth taking.

There was bound to be an overnight train to Rennes. If he

went straight to the Gare Montparnasse, he could book a sleeper, and then there'd be plenty of time for dinner before boarding – he'd heard of a new restaurant that rather appealed. He'd be in Rennes bright and early in the morning, with plenty of time to locate the address and talk to Artaud's ex-wife. Then grab a spot of lunch (Brittany: seafood, he thought, with mounting enthusiasm), and back to Paris on the early afternoon train.

He thought that seemed a pretty good plan.

To the north, lightning whitened the sky and silhouetted the hills. And again: eerie, silent lightning, stabbing at the flanks of Mont Ventoux, too distant for its thunder to be heard.

'I wish it would rain,' said Moira, and at three in the morning it did. The thunder came first, jolting awake all those who had managed to sleep in the cloying heat. The storm raged overhead for an hour in dry fury, then the rain began. It came down like pile-drivers, battering the roof-tiles, gushing from the gutters like Niagara.

It rained until five thirty and then stopped, just like that. By the time the sun had been up an hour, it might not have rained at all. The water was sucked into the thirsty soil, filtered through the limestone into hypogeal caverns, and what remained was burnt off in a fleeting mist. The sky was blue again.

At first sight, there seemed to be dew on the roadside verges. Closer inspection revealed a host of tiny, pearl-white snails, encrusting every blade of dried grass, every stalk of wild fennel. Chiara, curious, popped one into her mouth, but nothing of interest transpired, so she spat it out again. The sun rose higher, taking the temperature with it.

The address that Albuisson had been given by Danielle Jouvet was a small apartment building not far from the centre of Rennes. He found the right apartment easily enough, but the doorbell, when he pressed it, rang hollow and unheard.

It looked as though his luck had run out. The Brasseurs were on vacation after all. He cursed beneath his breath. Then a door along the corridor opened, and a sharp-faced blonde looked out.

'Who you looking for?'

'I was hoping to find Madame Brasseur,' he said.

The woman inspected him suspiciously. 'What do you want with her?'

'Police.' He showed his ID.

She became simultaneously defensive and intrigued. 'Nothing serious, I hope.'

'No, no,' he said, reassuringly. 'Just a formality. I suppose they're on holiday, are they?'

'No, they've gone.'

'Gone?'

'Moved out, and the new people haven't moved in yet.'

'Ah. You don't by any chance have their new address, do you?'

She hesitated, deciding whether to tell him. Eventually, she said: 'Yes, they left it with me, in case there was any mail to be forwarded. Hang on, I'll fetch it.'

He was afraid it would turn out that the Brasseurs had moved to yet another far-flung corner of the country, and relieved when he saw that the new address was also in Rennes. He found it in a half-finished estate on the outskirts of the town: a maze of near-identical little *pavillons*, each of them just far enough from the next to qualify for that most desirable appellation, the *maison individuelle*.

The Brasseur house still had a newly built rawness about it, a smell of damp plaster and sawdust. The little garden was no more than a patch of rough earth, bare but for a sprinkling of newly sprouted weeds and a toddler's red tricycle, upside-down. Albuisson walked up the steps to the front door, and rang the bell.

Marie-Christine Brasseur was a woman disappointed with life, and it showed. Even her smile was sour. She was heavy, in a sack-shaped cotton frock, and when she walked she barely raised her feet from the ground. Albuisson identified himself, assured her that there was no cause for concern, that he'd just like to ask her some questions.

'Is this to do with Jean-Michel?' she said instantly.

'In a way.'

'I might have known. If there's trouble, it's always something to do with him.'

In the background, he could hear the high-pitched voice of a young child, and then the sound of a baby crying.

The woman snapped, exasperated: 'Shit! I told Roger to keep Sophie out of the kitchen. Now she's gone and woken the baby. That was the first bit of peace I've had in twenty-four hours.'

Albuisson followed her into the house. It showed all the signs of very recent occupancy. Only the essential items of furniture had been unpacked and disposed haphazardly around the rooms; the rest remained in wooden crates, stacked in every corner.

In the kitchen, a stocky little girl, about two years old, was shrieking: 'Daddy, Daddy, *now*!' at a thin man in shorts, who was leaning over a bassinet, making ineffectual cooing noises.

His wife said, with undisguised scorn: 'You won't get anywhere doing that. She'll never stop unless you pick her up. Sophie, *shut up*! Just get outside this minute, before I thrash you.'

She snatched the screaming infant from the bassinet and rocked it against her shoulder. To Albuisson's untutored eye, it looked very young, no more than a couple of months old. Gradually, its screams subsided. She gave its rear an exploratory pat.

'She's wet,' she said to the hapless husband. 'You'd better go and change her.'

He meekly took the baby to some other part of the house.

'Men!' said his wife. 'Clueless, the lot of them.' She turned to Albuisson. 'Now, what do *you* want?'

'I'm trying to trace your ex-husband,' he said. 'I thought you might be able to tell me where he is.'

She gave a bitter little laugh. 'Oh, I know where he is, all right – at least, I'm ninety-nine per cent sure. But it won't be much help to you. He's dead.'

'Dead?'

'Traffic accident – right outside his apartment. Silly fool stepped off the pavement, right in the path of a truck. Just like him; never did look where he was going.'

'How long ago was this?' said Albuisson.

'I don't know – about six months. I've a copy of the death certificate somewhere, if you want to have a look at it.'

'Thank you, yes, that would be useful.'

She shuffled to the door and shouted down the hallway: 'Roger! Where's that box of papers? All that legal stuff?'

'In the living-room, next to the phone.'

The death certificate was unequivocal. Jean-Michel Artaud had died of cranial injuries on the 16th of February that year.

'We needed the certificate to sort out the will,' his ex-wife said. 'There was quite a bit of money, actually. Not that I wanted anything to do with it. He was always trying to give money to the boys while he was alive, but I wouldn't let him. I wasn't having him buying their affection – and anyway, with him, you never knew where it had come from. He saved it all up, though, put it in trust funds or something, so they'd inherit it when he died. And there was nothing I could do to stop that.'

Albuisson made a note of the details on the certificate. 'Do your sons live here?' he said.

'No. When we moved to Rennes, they stayed behind with my parents. We gave them the choice, and that's what they wanted. It was only to be expected; they didn't want to be dragged away from their schools and their friends. They'd been uprooted once, when we left Paris; they didn't want to go through it all again. Anyway, they're big enough to look after themselves now.'

Roger wearily returned, looking as though he had been wrestling a bear rather than changing a baby. He was pale and freckled; probably younger than his wife, Albuisson judged, though thinning hair made him look older.

'I put her in the cot,' he said. 'She's sleeping.'

'Well, hallelujah! Two minutes' silence before the next outburst, I expect.'

'I'll be on my way, then, and leave you in peace,' said Albuisson, not wishing to be there any longer than he had to.

The woman accompanied him to the door. He said: 'Thanks for your help. It's lucky I managed to find you at home. It being August, I was afraid you'd be away on holiday.'

'Holiday? Huh! With a new house and a new baby? Even if we had the time, we haven't got the money. The odd day trip to the coast, so Sophie can play on the beach; that's about it for this summer.'

'How old is the baby?'

'Just coming up to two months.'

'And the little girl?'

'Two-and-a-half – and a proper little green-eyed monster these days. She used to be such a sweet little thing. But then I was in hospital for six weeks with the other one, you see – problems with blood pressure – and Sophie thought I'd abandoned her. She really resents the baby, forever tormenting her; I have to watch her every minute. I suppose she'll grow out of it, eventually.' She sighed heavily. 'Children, I don't know; why do we bother?'

As he walked to the gate, Albuisson heard the sound of a baby, crying.

A big round bass voice boomed down the police station corridor.

'Georges, you old bastard! What are you doing here?'

And Albuisson grinned with genuine delight. A day that had started well, but then gone rapidly downhill, had finally been redeemed by a most serendipitous coincidence.

The Brasseurs' change of address had prolonged the morning's project, so lunch was rather later than intended; and at the restaurant he had ill-advisedly selected, the service was so slow that he had time for nothing more than a plate of unremarkable *crevettes*, gulped in haste, before cancelling the rest of his order and dashing for the train.

All the way back to Paris, he had suffered alternately from indigestion and frustration: a wild-goose chase round half of France, only to find that, at the time of Claude Chavanac's car crash, the three most promising suspects had been, respectively, dead for four months, confined to hospital, and walled up in a monastery.

Square one. Again.

As the train was drawing into the station, he had checked the railway timetable. If he had hurried, he could just about have made it across town in time to catch the next train home. But it was too hot to hurry, and there would be another train in a couple of hours. It wouldn't get him home until late, but it would do. In the meantime, he wanted to satisfy himself that Jean-Michel Artaud was well and truly dead. Clutching at straws, perhaps, but there was always a chance . . .

No point in looking for a grave; according to Artaud's ex-wife, the body had been cremated. ('You wouldn't catch me paying for a burial plot,' she'd said. 'As far as I'm concerned, they could have chucked him out with the rubbish.') But the death certificate had given him Artaud's last address, and it was there that the fatal accident had occurred. From that, he could work out which police station would have dealt with the incident.

And this was where the serendipitous coincidence came in. He had found the station, and begun to explain his query to the desk officer; and at that very moment Theo Haldemans came out of his office and recognized him.

He and Theo went back a long way. They were at college together. They had worked together. Most important of all, they had *dined* together. Theo shared Albuisson's passion for food, though on him it didn't show so much; the effects were more thinly distributed over a larger area. He was big and square, with the fair pigmentation of his Dutch ancestors, though in every other respect he was as French as they come. Paris seemed to suit him; he looked in fine fettle.

He poked Albuisson in the paunch. 'I see you've been eating well.'

'Not well enough, I'm afraid,' said Albuisson, recounting his recent gastronomic disappointments: the abbreviated lunch, and last night's meal – the restaurant that had seemed so promising on paper had turned out to be full of loud Americans, and the menu adulterated accordingly.

'That's Paris in August for you,' said Theo. 'The restaurants are all either closed or full of tourists. You must make up for it tonight. Come and eat with us. I'll call Lisette; I'm sure she can make the meal stretch to three.'

In Albuisson's experience, Lisette Haldemans' meals would readily stretch to half a dozen, even by his demanding standards; and her cooking, if not quite as good as his wife's, came a pretty close second.

He was sorely tempted, but he said: 'No, I've got a train to catch.'

'There'll be another one. You can stay at our place overnight, and catch the first train in the morning. Come on, why not? Lisette would love to see you.'

Well, Albuisson reasoned, it would be impolite to refuse.

'Now,' Theo said, 'what's this traffic accident you're looking into?'

Albuisson explained. Theo took control; the records were found; the officer in charge was found. Everything was in order.

'Who identified the body?' Albuisson enquired.

'One of the victim's sons,' said the officer in charge.

'What was he doing here? According to his mother, the sons live with their grandparents out in the country somewhere.'

'Well, maybe so, sir, but this one was living in Paris at the time.'

'I see. And he recognized his father? He presumably hadn't seen him since childhood; their mother seems to have done everything she could to keep his sons away from him.'

'Kids remember things, though. In any case, that wasn't the only identification. A neighbour identified the victim at the scene of the accident, and there were various forms of identification on the body.'

'So there couldn't have been any mistake?'

'I don't think so.'

Theo Haldemans patted Albuisson on the shoulder. 'Never mind,' he said. 'I'll phone Lisette to let her know we're coming, and then we'll have a couple of drinks on the way home.'

A few aperitifs at a congenial bar put Albuisson in a better frame of mind. Theo told him some good stories – cases he'd been working on, news of mutual acquaintances – and Albuisson told Theo about the frustrations of the Chavanac case.

'Every logical line of enquiry leads to a dead end,' he complained. 'People with motives have alibis; people without alibis have no motives. All I'm left with now is the contemplative monk and the Hippopotamus, and God only knows where she is.'

'Hippopotamus?' said Theo, intrigued.

Albuisson explained: 'Woman the size of a house, plenty of money, goes around in a white Merc with a midget. No known connection with Chavanac, no conceivable motive; but as soon as I turned up in Provence she disappeared without trace – which is no mean feat for a woman that size. It could have been coincidence, but I doubt it. She supposedly lives here in Paris, but we can't find her. She gave several different addresses, and none of them exists.'

'What did she call herself?'

'De Sousa – but that's probably false as well.'

And Theo started to laugh.

19

'We can forget the Hippopotamus,' said Albuisson, down a crackly telephone line.

'What? Where are you calling from?' said Andrieu.

'I'm on the TGV to Lyon.'

'Oh. And what's this about the Hippopotamus?'

'Madeleine de Sousa,' said Albuisson, ' – alias Roxanne Lefarge, Louise Delacroix and heaven knows what else – is a tart.'

'A *tart*?' said Andrieu, incredulously. He looked at the photographs pinned up by his desk; the idea was too gruesome to contemplate.

'A tart,' repeated Albuisson. 'And a very successful one, at that. Made a fair packet, in her time. Of course, she may have been thinner in those days. Anyway, once she'd made enough money she set up her own bordello – a high-class establishment, by all accounts, patronized by the rich and famous. In fact, she became quite rich and famous herself.'

'So how come we couldn't find her? She must be on police files somewhere, but none of my contacts in Paris had heard of her.'

'She's been in apparently respectable retirement for a good few years now – a very shrewd woman, despite appearances; she sold out at a profit while the going was good. Your contacts are probably too young to have known her in her prime, and they didn't look far enough back in the files. Or else the files have been doctored; that wouldn't surprise me. I gather she had a certain amount of influence in official circles – it wasn't just the rich and famous who enjoyed her services, if you get my drift.'

'Then how did you find out about her?'

'My contacts in the Paris police are rather older than yours. One of them remembers her from the old days, and he had an idea where I might find her.'

'What about the midget: what's he? Her pimp?'

'No,' said Albuisson, 'he's her son.'

'Her *son*?' Andrieu sniggered. 'It's hard to see the family resemblance.'

'Perhaps being raised in a whorehouse stunts your growth. What it certainly does is teach you to spot a policeman a kilometre away – which would explain why they left Provence. When de Sousa junior saw me sniffing round the Merc, he got the wind up. He scuttled back to their villa, alerted Mama, and they bolted.'

'So their disappearance had nothing to do with the Chavanac case?'

'It seems not. They barely knew the Chavanacs – and they couldn't have had anything to do with the events in St-Geraud; they can prove they were abroad at the time. They'd no idea what I was doing in Provence, but as I was showing an interest in their car, they were afraid it must be something to do with them.'

'But if she's respectable now, what did they have to be afraid of?'

'There's always something, with people like that. However well they've covered their tracks, they never stop looking over their shoulders.'

'So what do we do now?'

'Well, I'm on my way to a monastery.'

'Things are not that bad, are they?' said Andrieu.

The TGV whisked Albuisson briskly from Paris to Lyon and a fortuitously well-timed connection with a fast train to Grenoble. From there he took a taxi up into the tree-clad slopes of the Chartreuse. It was still very hot, even here, but the air was fresher; above the trees, he caught an occasional glimpse of sharp white peaks. The taxi twisted and turned along steep, narrow roads and came to a halt by a gate.

'Is this it?' he said.

He'd been expecting something grander, ancient stones and sanctity; this place looked like a holiday camp – a bright green pasture ringed with mountains and scattered with little wooden cabins. A rutted track led to a larger building at the distant end of the pasture, a flat single-storey affair, like something you might see on an industrial estate.

The gate was locked. On the right-hand gatepost there was a plain iron cross, a mailbox and a bellpush. Albuisson pushed it.

'You want me to wait?' said the taxi-driver.

'Yes.' He didn't fancy being stuck out here without transport.

Time passed, though it hardly seemed that way. The taxi-driver switched off the engine and lit a cigarette. The only sounds were the humming of insects and the tinkling of bells from unseen flocks. At length, a figure came into view. It proceeded in an unhurried fashion along the track towards the gate; as it approached, it resolved into a youngish man dressed in a long, plain robe.

Albuisson explained his business; the man listened in passive silence. It was odd, like talking to an answerphone: no questions, no feedback, just pouring words into a void. When he'd finished, the man inclined his head in acknowledgement, and spoke for the first time.

'Please wait here,' he said.

He went back the way he had come, walking at a measured pace, neither fast nor slow. Albuisson turned to the taxi-driver; the taxi-driver shrugged.

'Funny lot,' he said. 'Can't see the point of it, myself.'

The man could be seen entering the larger building. Presently, he reappeared and walked towards one of the cabins; when he came out, there was a second man with him, and they both came towards the gate.

'This is Brother Gabriel,' the first man said. 'He's willing to speak to you, and our Superior has given his permission.' He produced a key from somewhere within his robe, and unlocked the gate. 'Come in, please.'

Albuisson was escorted to the cabin closest to the gate.

'I'll wait outside,' said the first monk. He closed the door behind him.

Inside, the air was hot and dense and dusty, with a faint barnyard smell. There was a small table and four folding chairs; a wooden cross hung on the wall. Brother Gabriel unfolded two of the chairs, placed them on either side of the table and waited for the visitor to sit before he followed suit.

'I take it you are – that is, you were – Richard Dullin,' Albuisson said.

'That's right.'

'How long have you been here?'

'Four years. Or is it five? I don't know; time isn't that important here.'

The barnyard smell was getting stronger. It was, Albuisson realized, emanating from Brother Gabriel.

'What do you do here?' he said.

'We pray. And we each have our duties. I look after the goats.'

'Ah,' said Albuisson. That would explain it. 'And do none of you ever leave the monastery?'

'Our Superior has to go out into the world from time to time – sadly, in this day and age, we can't cut ourselves off completely. We're as self-sufficient as we can be, but there are still matters out there that have to be dealt with. And if one of us is seriously ill he may have to go to a hospital. We're permitted to go out in exceptional circumstances – the funeral of a close family member, things like that – but that's at the discretion of our Superior.'

'Have you ever been out?'

'No, never. I haven't set foot beyond that gate since I arrived – and never wanted to.'

'Do you have any contact with people outside?'

'No. Correspondence is allowed, but there's no one I'd want to write to.'

'You have no family?'

'No.'

The aroma of goat was becoming overwhelming. Albuisson said: 'I assume your, er, colleague . . .'

'Brother Martin.'

'Brother Martin, yes; I assume he told you why I'm here.'

'The Grissot case.'

'Yes. I'll try to keep it brief; I imagine it's not something you'd wish to dwell on.'

'Not at all. It was my salvation; it led me here. I give thanks for it daily.'

'I see. Well, I've been talking to some of the other people involved in the case, and . . .'

Brother Gabriel's face twisted, torn between pious restraint and human curiosity. Curiosity prevailed.

'Have you spoken to Artaud?' he said.

'Er, no. I suppose you wouldn't have heard: he's dead.'

'Dead? When? How did he die?'

'Earlier this year. He was knocked down in the street.'

'He always was careless. Thank you for telling me. I shall pray for him. I suppose you've seen Jouvet?'

'Yes.'

'I met him once or twice after I came out of prison. I went to his house; his wife was very kind. Did you see her? How is she?'

'She seemed well. They're separated, though.'

'Are they? I'm not surprised. Now he'll be free to have all the girls he wants.'

'Girls?'

'Didn't you know? He was notorious. No typist was safe in our office – especially the younger ones. I think he was afraid of growing old; he saw these girls as a sort of elixir of youth. Of course, I may be maligning him. It's so long since I've seen him; he may have changed.'

Albuisson suspected not, remembering the panties on the bathroom floor.

'And Claude Chavanac,' the man said, 'he was another womanizer – though his range was somewhat wider. As a student, I remember, he had an affair with a woman professor who must have been twice his age. Then he married that English girl – are they still together?'

'Yes. They have two children.'

'I thank God I had no children. Not that I shun responsibility. I have my goats: I look after them, I care for them, I love them as God's creatures – but I impose nothing upon them, you see?

It's different with children; we pass our burdens on to them. I'd rather carry my own.'

'How did you and Artaud feel about Chavanac after the Grissot trial? Were you angry that he failed to get you acquitted?'

'Not really. He had a fairly hopeless task; the evidence was stacked against us.'

'But Jouvet was acquitted.'

'He had a better case.'

'You mean he wasn't guilty?'

'I mean there was less evidence against him.'

'Have you had any contact with Chavanac since the trial?'

'No.'

There seemed little more to be said. Perhaps he should have persisted in his questioning, but the combination of mounting claustrophobia and intensifying goat was becoming unbearable. He terminated the interview and escaped into the fresh air.

Brother Martin escorted him back to the road. Albuisson remarked: 'Brother Gabriel tells me he's been here five years and never once been beyond this gate.'

'That's right. I've been here seven years, myself, and I've only been out once – to have a wisdom tooth extracted. Gabriel's never been out at all. We have no desire to leave, you see.' He turned the key. 'This lock isn't here to keep us in. It's to keep others out.'

He pushed open the gate, and Albuisson was back in the real world.

A waste of time? he pondered, waiting on the platform at Clermont-Ferrand for the train that would take him home to St-Geraud. It was late, he was tired, he was famished. A whole day chasing round the country for the sake of a fifteen-minute conversation that told him very little indeed – except that, like all the other suspects, Richard Dullin seemed well and truly out of the picture.

Dullin – he found it hard to think of the man as Brother Gabriel – had seemed genuine when he said the Grissot case was his salvation. Ironic, really: like Philippe Rocard, he saw his misfortune as a blessing in disguise; if anything, there was gratitude rather than resentment. And there seemed no reason to doubt Dullin's claim, confirmed by his fellow monk, that he hadn't been out of the monastery in years.

So, there: another tin duck out of the firing line. What now?

20

Andrieu doodled dispiritedly on the photograph in front of him. It was a blow-up of one of the shots at the *pétanque* match; with a felt-tipped pen, he had given Claude a moustache and Moira a cowboy hat. Philippe Rocard had regained a full head of hair, and his wife was about to be embellished in a vaguely pornographic manner when Albuisson appeared.

'What are you doing?' he said.

Andrieu hastily amended his scribbles.

'I'm, er, scrubbing out the people we've eliminated from the enquiry,' he improvised, 'just to see what we're left with.' He blanked out various faces. 'And the answer is: not a lot. I've checked out that old couple, the Massons; as we thought, he was in hospital in Orléans at the time of the St-Geraud goings-on, and according to the hospital staff, his wife was camped by his bedside day and night. So that rules them out – not that they were very likely suspects in the first place. Which leaves just the so-called Newlyweds. Are they worth investigating?'

'On the face of it, no – they're too young, and they've got an alibi for at least one of the incidents. But for the sake of completeness, I suppose we ought to make a few enquiries. Unfortunately, we don't even know their names. Zoe Chavanac's been asking around, but she says the whole village refers to them as the Newlyweds. They don't mix much with the other people there; even the woman whose house they're renting doesn't know what they're called. She told Zoe they'd arrived on spec and paid in advance, in cash. If they'd booked ahead, or paid by cheque, she'd have got their name and address, but as it was, she didn't bother.'

'Couldn't somebody just ask them what their names are?'

'I don't want to arouse their suspicions.'

'Has it occurred to you,' Andrieu said, 'that the person we're looking for may have had his suspicions aroused already? Look at the dates: there were three incidents in succession between the 7th and the 12th of this month – but since then, there's been nothing, and it's now the 24th. Maybe he's got cold feet or gone to ground; maybe he's not even in Provence any more.'

'That's possible,' Albuisson admitted. 'But there may be other reasons. The incidents don't seem to be scheduled; they're opportunistic. It may be that there just haven't been any opportunities lately – especially if the Chavanacs are being more careful and keeping their eyes open.'

'Well, okay. But if we don't even have a name for these two kids, where do we start?'

'I've got the *matriculation* details from their motor bike, and the name of the dealer in Limoges who sold it. I suggest we start there.'

'Are you going to do it, or shall I?'

'You do it. I have to visit my mother.'

Madame Albuisson senior was almost perfectly spherical. She was considerably shorter than her son, but her other dimensions were similar. Her little house was full of cooking smells.

'I was beginning to think you'd forgotten where I live,' she said accusingly, as he stooped to plant a kiss on her cushiony cheek.

He said: 'I've been busy. I had to go to Provence, and then Paris . . .'

'So *she* told me.'

She was Madame Albuisson junior. He was perpetually perplexed by his mother's hostility towards her. If he'd married some flighty glamourpuss or pushy career woman, then he could have understood it. But his wife did all the things that his mother considered right and proper for a woman: she cooked, she sewed, she knitted, she polished; she tended the garden and kept chickens and ducks at the bottom of it. What more could any mother want of a daughter-in-law? It was a mystery to him.

He was ushered through the little parlour, crammed with a

lifetime's accumulation of furniture – his mother hated to throw anything away – and into the kitchen, where pans were simmering.

'Sit down. Lunch isn't quite ready,' she said. She picked up an envelope from the dresser and put it on the table in front of him. 'These are the photographs I told you about – you know, the old ones of your father that Denise Brunet gave me.'

He opened the envelope and slid out the photographs. His father smiled out of them, hardly recognizable, younger than he'd ever known him. He pulled out two.

'These are very good,' he said. 'Were these the ones you wanted to get framed?'

'Yes. They're nice, aren't they?'

'I'll take them with me. I know a man who does picture framing.'

'Will it be expensive?' (His mother lived up to the Auvergnat stereotype; the idea of money as something to be spent was a concept she had never entirely come to terms with.)

'No, I shouldn't think so.' (Because down at headquarters everyone knows that the picture framer on the corner does a spot of fencing, too, but a blind eye gets turned in exchange for the odd bit of information and a couple of pictures framed now and then.)

'She was on the phone again the other day, you know.' his mother said.

'Who was?'

'Denise Brunet. That poor woman, what she must be going through.'

'Why? What's happened?'

'It's her boy, Denis; seems to have got himself into a spot of bother. I don't know what it's all about, some property deal or something; she did say, but it made no sense to me, all this financial business. All I know is, it looks like he's been up to no good with someone else's money, and there's something to do with politicians and bribes being paid . . .'

'I haven't heard anything about this.'

'It hasn't come out into the open yet.'

'Then why was she telling you about it?'

'She wanted to talk to someone she could trust. Old friends are the best, she says, you know where you are with them.'

And smart Paris friends wouldn't want to know, he thought.

'Anyway, it'll all be public knowledge in a few days. She says Denis is putting his affairs in order, and then he's going to turn himself over to the authorities.'

'Is Albert involved?'

'She didn't exactly say, but I think he might be. Something to do with that new house of theirs – Denis handled the purchase, you see.'

His mother lifted the lid of a pan and stirred.

'There, that's ready. And there's *clafoutis* in the oven for later; you like that.'

He had expressed a passion for *clafoutis* at the age of nine, and his mother had been stuffing him with it ever since.

'I'll bet it's lighter than *hers*, too,' she said.

He was itching to know more of what Denise Brunet had said, but the opportunity was gone. His mother had veered off in another direction, and he knew from experience that it would be pointless to attempt to bring her back; he would have to find out some other way. Right now, he was expected to give his full attention to lunch.

'Good lunch?' said Andrieu, insubordinately, with an ostentatious glance at his watch as Albuisson reappeared shortly after four o'clock.

'Indeed. Most illuminating,' said Albuisson, mysteriously. 'Have you had any luck with that motor bike?'

'Yes. It's registered to one Gregoire Louisot. I got on to the dealer in Limoges; he sold the bike round about Easter. He remembered the sale, he said, because it was this kid poking around an expensive machine, asking all kinds of questions – practically had the engine to bits in the showroom – and he thought he must be up to something, because he looked like he didn't have two francs to rub together. Then he reached inside his jacket and pulled out a wad – enough to pay for the bike there and then, all in readies. Naturally, the dealer was a bit suspicious, but the kid said the money came from his dad, and he could phone the bank and check up if he wanted to. So the dealer phoned the bank; they said the money was good, and he sold the kid the bike.'

'Anything else?'

'Well, the dealer still had the kid's details on file, including a phone number, so I phoned it. I pretended to be a *flic*, checking out what seemed to be an error on the registration documents. The phone's in the name of a M. Bernard Louisot – presumably Gregoire's father. I looked up the place on the map – it's a small village, just east of Confolens. When I called the number, someone called Emil answered; said he was Gregoire's brother. According to him, Gregoire still officially lives there, but he's not around much these days; he's studying engineering, at a college in Paris. His brother was aware he was on holiday at the moment, but he didn't know where.

'He gave me Gregoire's phone number in Paris, though. So I called that, and talked to his flat-mate. He doesn't know where Gregoire is, either; says he just took off with some girl. He didn't know much about her, except that her first name's Laurence. He said she's someone Gregoire knew in the past but hadn't seen for a long time; then they met up by chance at a party about four or five months ago, and there was a whirlwind romance.

'He seemed a bit taken aback about that. It appears this Gregoire's a great romantic, but never had a lot of luck with women – which doesn't surprise me, if these photographs are anything to go by. And he's a bit of a country bumpkin, whereas she's a hardboiled Parisienne, according to the flat-mate; he reckoned it must have been the motor bike that pulled her. I think I detected a touch of jealousy – though whether that was for the girl or the bike, I wouldn't like to say. He didn't seem to know they were married – he referred to her all the way through as Gregoire's girlfriend, not his wife.'

'Maybe they're *not* married,' said Albuisson. 'Either that, or they got hitched without letting anyone know. Perhaps they thought their families wouldn't approve. Still, at least now we have names for them – but what's the connection with Chavanac?'

'Search me. But there's one more lead to follow: Gregoire's college.'

'I'd have thought it would be closed for the summer.'

'Yes, but the flat-mate's on the same course as Gregoire, and he knew the home phone number for one of their tutors.

Assuming he's not on holiday, he may be able to answer some questions – I'm just trying to invent a convincing excuse to explain why I'm asking them, without giving the game away. I think I need a coffee to stimulate the creative process. How about you?'

Andrieu made terrible coffee. 'I'll get it,' Albuisson said.

There was a coffee machine in the corridor, and pots of filter coffee that sat around on hotplates and tasted like a bonfire left out in the rain. Albuisson shunned all such abominations. He made his own coffee, freshly ground, in his own *cafetière*, and poured two cups – china, not paper.

Privately, Andrieu preferred the stuff from the machine; cops should be standing up drinking bad coffee from cardboard in corridors, not sitting sipping politely from china with their little fingers stuck up in the air. But he couldn't bring himself to tell Albuisson that, so he accepted the cup that was offered.

Albuisson said: 'I went to see Albert Brunet this afternoon.'

'Oh?'

'And I found out what it was he was afraid of – why he interfered with our investigation.'

'So there *was* something going on, after all?'

'His son's involved in a property scandal. I don't know all the ins and outs of it, but Albert's caught up in it, too, to some extent. There was some tricky deal that enabled him to pick up his grand new house for a fraction of what it's worth.'

'I wouldn't have thought he was that hard up.'

'He's not. Apart from anything else, when he was in Paris, he owned a huge apartment in one of the posh *arrondissements*; with the money he got for that, he could have bought a palace down here. But, like I said once before: he doesn't do these things because he needs to; he does them because he can. He'd also used his influence to swing a few political decisions in his son's favour – something to do with a big hypermarket development scheme – and it would seem that a certain amount of money changed hands to oil the wheels.'

Andrieu was underwhelmed. 'That sort of thing goes on all the time.'

'Yes, I know; and everyone turns a blind eye. But it can still come unstuck if things go wrong. There's a recession on; Denis Brunet had overstretched himself. There was a problem with money, bad debts. He and Albert both knew that if the business collapsed there'd be an enquiry, and all sorts of nasty secrets would come creeping out of the woodwork. If he could have got a rescue package together, he might have got away with it – but to do that he had to convince the banks that he was squeaky-clean. He couldn't afford to have anyone nosing around his affairs – or his father's.'

Now it was getting more interesting. 'Then we were right in the first place,' Andrieu said. 'Albert Brunet *was* afraid of Claude Chavanac!'

'Wrong.'

'Wrong? But it's obvious – even if he wasn't concerned about himself, he'd go to any lengths to protect his son.'

'Right. But not against Claude Chavanac.'

'Then who?'

'Us.'

'Us?'

'Exactly. Back in June, at the time of the car crash, they didn't think they had anything to be afraid of. Denis didn't know his business was in trouble till July, when one of his partners unexpectedly went bankrupt. It was only after that – late July, early August – that he started talking to the banks. And then we turned up, investigating his father.'

'But we were investigating something completely different.'

'I know; but that didn't matter. We were trying to find out if Brunet had anything to hide – and he did. We may have started out with the wrong question, but we were in danger of coming up with the right answer.'

'So Brunet got Parrilaud to switch us off.'

'That's right. It did him no good in the end, though. The banks refused to back Denis anyway – on straight financial grounds, regardless of any funny business. So the company will go down, the truth will come out – well, some of it – and there's at least a possibility that Brunet's fine new homestead is going to end up in the hands of the creditors. It'll be in all the papers in a few days.'

Andrieu frowned, curious. 'So how come you know about it now?'

Albuisson beamed. 'I got it from a little old lady,' he said.

A pity, really, Andrieu thought. He would have liked it to be Brunet, just for the pleasure of seeing the smug old bastard's face when they collared him; serve him right for screwing up their investigation – and smoothie-chops Parrilaud would have had some explaining to do. And, even when the evidence had swung against Brunet, there had still been the lingering possibility that something would turn up to point them back in his direction. But now even that was gone.

So: back to the spotty-faced kid on the motor bike. Not much of a suspect at all. The only points in his favour seemed to be his presence in Provence, plus the fact that he apparently knew something about motor mechanics, so maybe he'd have the know-how to fiddle with Chavanac's brakes. But against that, there was no apparent motive, and no obvious access to a computer and printer; he had an alibi for one of the events in Provence, and there was nothing to place him in the Auvergne at the time of the earlier incidents.

Andrieu reached for the phone and once again dialled the number he'd been given for Gregoire Louisot's tutor. He'd already tried several times without success, but this time he was in luck.

'Is that Michel Rostov?'

'Yes. Who is this?'

'Police. You have a student called Gregoire Louisot?'

'Yes.' The voice sounded concerned. 'Is he in some sort of trouble?'

'Would you expect him to be?'

Ironic laughter. 'Students are always in trouble, of one kind or another.'

'Well, I'm not sure if he's in trouble or not; that's why I'm calling. I can't get hold of him directly; he's on holiday and nobody seems to know where. His family haven't seen him for several months, and his flat-mate hasn't seen him for weeks – he's the one who gave me your number.'

'What's the problem?'

Andrieu reeled out the story he'd invented: a motor bike, he said, had been involved in an incident near St-Geraud on the 9th of June. A witness had noted part of the *matriculation*; the computer had come up with all the possible combinations of letters and numbers that would match the witness statement, and picked out the ones that were attached to motor bikes. Now all he had to do was check up on the owners of each of those bikes, to see if they'd been in the area at the time. Gregoire Louisot, he said, was the next on his list.

Rostov seemed to have bought the story. 'When did you say this was?' he said.

'The 9th of June. It was a Thursday.'

'Well, in that case, you can cross Gregoire off your list. On the 9th of June – in fact, the whole of that week – he was taking exams here in Paris.'

'You're quite definite about that?'

'I saw him in the examination rooms. I marked some of his papers. In fact, on the Thursday, if I remember rightly – just let me check my diary; yes: he had his presentation that afternoon. Each student has to present the results of his special dissertation project to a panel of examiners. He did a very good presentation, in fact. He'd been studying stress tolerance in various structural materials – the extent to which you can bend or distort them under difficult conditions.'

'You were one of the examiners, I take it.'

'Yes, myself and two other members of staff.'

'And how long did the presentation last?'

'About two hours, from two thirty to four thirty.'

'Presumably, the college records would confirm all this?'

'Of course.'

Well, there goes another bright idea, thought Andrieu.

Zoe wandered into the kitchen to prepare the evening meal. She dismantled a lettuce, chopped a few random vegetables, and wrapped all the trimmings in a page from yesterday's newspaper.

Moira had abandoned her collection of papers to take home. Hugo had protested that, even in the back of a Volvo, capacity was not unlimited, and the space occupied by a pile of old newspapers could perhaps be more profitably used to transport another case or two of Côtes du Ventoux. Even Moira could appreciate the merits of this argument.

The remains of the newspaper slid off the table; Zoe bent to pick it up. It had fallen open at the advertising section – the section they had all been avoiding for over a week now, since Albuisson's visit.

At first, everyone had been on edge, but they were beginning to relax a little now. There had been no more incidents; perhaps it was over. Under a slate-grey northern sky the threat might have seemed more real, but when the sun shone and everyone around was in holiday mood, it was easy to believe that all was well with the world. Checking the advertisements somehow seemed like tempting fate. But with the paper there, open, in front of her, Zoe's glance was drawn irresistibly down the page.

And there, in the middle of the small ads, it said: 'C.C.: Still thinking of you.'

21

'How come no one noticed at the newspaper office?' said Andrieu. 'I thought they were supposed to be keeping a look-out for any more ads.'

Albuisson said: 'They were. They missed it. They were full of apologies.'

As soon as he got the phone call from Claude Chavanac, he'd been on to the newspaper's head office. They'd been assiduously checking all the personal ads as they came in; but then someone just back from holiday, knowing nothing about the Chavanac affair, had let the latest ad slip through the net.

'We can't really blame them,' Albuisson said, philosophically. 'Their job is to print newspapers, not to do police work. They're checking now to find out how the ad came in, if it was the same as all the others. In the meantime, the question is – why?'

'Why what?'

'Why was the ad placed? Nothing's happened.'

'I don't know. Could it be some kind of psychological

warfare? I read somewhere that if you hit someone and ring a bell at the same time, and you keep doing it often enough, then eventually you don't even have to hit them; you can just ring the bell on its own and it has the same effect.'

'Pavlovian response,' said Albuisson.

'If you say so.'

'I'm not altogether convinced.'

'Well, what's your explanation?'

Good question. Albuisson put it to Maria Zwitalska, over lunch.

She looked like someone's granny: white-haired, clad in knitting and deceptively cuddly. In fact, she was an authority on criminal psychology, with a sharp tongue and an alphabet of qualifications trailing after her name. Police forces all over France called on her services; her particular area of expertise lay in the analysis of written materials – ransom notes and poison-pen letters; taunting messages from cocksure criminals; witness statements and dubious confessions.

She was also a sucker for a good lunch. Between courses, Albuisson explained the circumstances, while she studied the text of the seven advertisements directed at Claude Chavanac, and a photocopy of the one original letter they had managed to retrieve.

'Curious,' she said. Despite her exotic name, which carried a certain cachet in psychological circles, she was Auvergnat born and bred, with an accent as strong as an old Cantal cheese.

'Why curious?' Albuisson asked.

'The wording of each of the first three ads is related in some way to the events. "Here's to the next time": that makes sense as the start of a sequence, a warning that something else is going to happen. "The scent of pine", as you've already identified, could refer both to burning wood – the fire – and to a death threat. And the third message – "You can never replace the irreplaceable": that connects quite neatly with the loss of the rare books. But the later ones have no particular connection – at least, none that I can see.'

Albuisson scanned the list: 'Just to let you know how I feel' after the Sunday lunch incident; 'I'll never forget you' for the drowning of the cat; 'The last ten years – I owe it all to you' after the falling rock. She was right; none of them directly reflected the events they had accompanied. As for the most recent – 'Still thinking of you' – there seemed to be no event for the words to reflect.

Albuisson put forward Andrieu's Pavlovian theory.

'It's possible,' she said. 'It depends what the sender of these messages is trying to achieve. Is it protracted psychological warfare, or is it real physical harm – perhaps even murder? Clearly, there is a psychological component, otherwise there'd be no point to the advertisements. If you simply want to do someone harm, you just do it. But are these events a means to an end – to trigger off a sense of fear or persecution that can then be sustained by other means? Or are they an end in themselves?'

'What do you think?'

'On this evidence, it's very hard to say. Both the events and the advertisements carry mixed messages. On the one hand, we have actions like the car crash and the falling rock, which are serious – potentially fatal, even. And on the other hand, we have the cancelled lunch reservation, which is nothing more than a prank. It may have been dressed up with macabre connotations – there's the reference to a death in the family – but in essence it's just a practical joke.

'As for the drowning – well, it was unpleasant for the cat, no doubt, and maybe unsettling for the children, but hardly in the same league as tampering with the brakes on someone's car. The other events – the fire and the break-in – fall somewhere between the two, harmful but not lethal.

'It suggests someone who's very mixed up and confused, who really doesn't know what he wants to achieve from all this. Either that, or he's deliberately setting out to create confusion – perhaps because he thinks it's more unsettling that way, or simply to make himself more difficult to identify.'

'If it's the latter, he's certainly succeeding,' said Albuisson. 'Tell me: you refer to this person as "he"; is there something that makes you think it's a man, rather than a woman?'

She chuckled. 'No, Georges; it's just this excellent lunch that's making my analysis sloppy. "He" is shorthand for he, she or it. There's really nothing in these phrases to indicate the sex of the writer. They're too short and stylised to tell us very much.'

'Do they tell us anything at all?'

'Well, apart from the first two, which are simply threats, there's the underlying message that this man, C.C., has caused the writer to suffer in some way, and now he or she intends to inflict a similar suffering in return. But there's no indication of the nature of the damage done – except perhaps, if we read a double meaning into the advertisement that came after the break-in, that whatever happened was irreversible, ineradicable; something was destroyed or taken away.'

'What about the reference to "ten years" in the third advertisement: what do you make of that? It's the only phrase that gives anything away – do you think that's intentional, or did the writer slip up?'

'I think it's intentional. These aren't long, rambling messages, and they're not composed on the spur of the moment. They're short and quite cleverly crafted, so that no one except the intended recipient would think they were anything other than what they purport to be. But the writer has a dilemma: on the one hand, the obvious need to preserve anonymity; on the other, the desire to make the target feel guilty – it's hard to do that, if he doesn't know what it is he's being blamed for. So the "ten years" may be a deliberate clue, to point him in the right direction. Or, of course, a deliberate red herring.'

'Do you think this person is a serious danger?'

'On the basis of these advertisements, I really couldn't say. But on the basis of what you've told me about what's happened, I'd have to say yes: obsessed and reckless, not too concerned if other people get in the firing line – but at the same time, very determined and measured. Some of the individual events would seem to be opportunistic, but the overall scheme is long-term and well planned. And then there's the delay of three or four days after each event before the advertisement appears.'

'Why do you think that is?'

'I don't know; perhaps to heighten the tension. What I do know is that it suggests a degree of deliberation and self-control.'

'Can we learn anything from the use of language, spelling or whatever? Is this an educated person?'

'I'd have to do a proper analysis to answer that; and there isn't much to go on. On the surface, one can say that there are no errors in the advertisements as published, but they may have been corrected by copy editors. No mistakes in the letter, either – but, again, that could be attributed to the spell-checker in the word processor, rather than the literacy of the writer. The false name, now: P. Bonnard – the painter, perhaps?'

'Painter?' Albuisson was not well acquainted with the visual arts.

'Pierre Bonnard; a Post-Impressionist.'

'Oh? Is that significant?'

'Being a Post-Impressionist? Probably not. But the choice of name, maybe. People find it surprisingly difficult to invent names; they often resort to using the names of real people. And they frequently draw them from an area of life they're familiar with – so, someone familiar with literature might use the name of a writer . . .'

'. . . and someone familiar with painting might use the name of a painter?'

'Precisely. Nothing too overt, of course – V. Van Gogh or P. Picasso would rather give the game away. But a commonplace name like Bonnard would be safe enough. Do any of your suspects have artistic connections?'

'What suspects?' said Albuisson, morosely.

'Oh dear, is it as bad as that? Never mind, cheer up; here comes the sweet trolley.'

Andrieu, heading back from a rather more modest lunch, thinking things through and paying insufficient attention to his driving, found himself stuck in the wrong lane. He indicated, and attempted to nose out, but the car in the next lane wouldn't give a centimetre; he turned to cast a malevolent glare at the driver – some rich git in a sports car, a Claude Chavanac clone.

And he thought: the car. We've been forgetting about the car.

In his mind, he'd put aside the investigation into what might have happened to Chavanac's car, in favour of more promising lines of enquiry. He'd filed it away as part of the Brunet investigation; and when Brunet was crossed off the list of suspects, he'd abandoned the car, too, without really thinking it through.

But that's dumb, he thought now. Whoever was responsible – whether it was Brunet or anyone else – they'd got at the car, somehow. But how, and when, and where?

Back at HQ – Albuisson still out, he noted – he found the crash investigation file and went through it again, hoping it might tell him something he didn't already know. But there was nothing. The garage mechanics' report, the accident investigators' report, Chavanac's own statement; they all hung together. It still appeared that the only time the car was vulnerable was in the few hours it was parked while Chavanac was at lunch.

Which led him back to the hotel staff. Albuisson had felt they were hiding something – but what? And how could he prise it out of them? There was nothing to go on, no evidence to wave under their noses, not even enough to bluff it out.

Unless . . .

He scrabbled through the file again, pulling out the separate documents. Here, the work report from the garage; at the top, the date, the job reference number, the *matriculation* of the car, and the *kilométrage*: 5012. And here, the investigators' report, with all the technical details, and the readings from the dashboard instruments; at the time of the crash, there were 5206 kilometres on the clock.

Andrieu found himself a map and a pencil and paper; mental arithmetic had never been his strong suit. After the car had left the garage, Chavanac had driven it straight home, a distance of only a few kilometres – ten at the outside. Then, on the day of the accident, he had driven it from there to St-Flour – about seventy-five kilometres, Andrieu estimated – and back again; thirty-five kilometres, roughly, to the scene of the crash.

Now, total those distances – ten plus seventy-five plus thirty-five gives a hundred and twenty – and add that to the 5012 kilometres on the garage work report; and what you get is 5132. Which is seventy-four kilometres less than the number on the clock at the time of the crash.

So, maybe there'd be a few extra kilometres in there somewhere. Maybe Chavanac took a detour, made a diversion. But seventy-four kilometres? If he'd left home after ten thirty and arrived at the hotel before twelve, and bearing in mind the nature of the roads in the area, it was hard to see how he'd have had the time to drive an extra seventy-four kilometres.

In which case: who did?

Andrieu took his time; didn't want to get there too early. It was just after six by the time he arrived at the hotel; glanced inside briefly, to make sure that she was there, and then hung around, waiting for the staff to change over to the evening shift. He lurked in a doorway as she came out, and caught up with her in the street.

'Hi,' he said brightly. 'Remember me?'

The woman turned nervously: the older receptionist, the one he'd always known was the weak link in the chain. It was clear from her expression that she remembered him all too well, and wished she didn't. She quickened her pace; he trotted along beside her.

'I thought we might have a quick chat,' he said.

'I've nothing more to say than what I've already said. I thought this was all finished with.'

'Why don't we go for a drink?' he suggested.

'I've got to get home. I've a meal to cook.'

'It won't take very long.'

'It'll take no time at all. I've got nothing to say.'

'Or we could go to the police station, if you prefer.'

She looked horrified. 'No. There's a place just down here.'

He followed her along a narrow side street and into a featureless little bar. Two men stood at the counter; a third played the computer game machine in the corner.

'What will you have?' Andrieu asked her.

'Salers-Cassis.'

She sat down at a table away from the window. He brought across her drink, and a Coke for himself. She listlessly stirred the lurid pinky-orange mixture with a plastic cocktail stick, and then drank it back in one. There was a nervous silence, punctuated by the mind-numbing electronic beeps of the video game.

'Now then,' he said. 'Tell me what happened with Claude Chavanac's car.'

'It was put in a car-park, and the keys were returned to the hotel; that's all I know.'

'So how did it clock up seventy-four kilometres while it was sitting in a car-park?'

Her face slipped. Got you! he thought.

'It was nothing to do with me,' she said.

'All the more reason for telling me what happened.'

She hesitated. 'Put some records on.'

Andrieu rummaged in his pocket for change, stuck a few coins in the jukebox and selected numbers at random. The voice of Johnny Hallyday filled the bar. He didn't like Johnny Hallyday.

He went back to the table.

The woman stared at her hands.

'They think I'm an old stick-in-the-mud, the rest of them,' she said. 'Goody-goody, sucking up to management. It's all right for them, they've got no responsibilities. I've got responsibilities. I need that job.' She fiddled with her empty glass, pushing it around the table top in tight little circles. 'They make my life a misery as it is. "Just teasing," they call it, if I say anything. "Don't get your knickers in a twist, it's only teasing." Well, there's teasing and teasing, I say. If they find out I've been talking to you . . .'

'There's no reason why they should.'

'Well,' the woman said, 'Jeanne and Gilbert – they're the two on the morning shift, they were on duty when Chavanac arrived that day. Gilbert really fancies Jeanne; he's always showing off in front of her, trying to impress her. So he parked the car, like he said, and when I arrived, he was chatting her up, telling her how flash this car was, and how he'd take her for a spin in it when they got off duty. And she was saying no, they couldn't, but Henri – that's the other doorman, the one on my shift – he was egging them on. So, when they went off duty, they took the keys and went out in the car – down the *autoroute,* with Gilbert showing off, as usual, driving at some ridiculous speed.'

'And?'

'Well, that's it, really. They took the car for a spin and then brought it back.'

'That's all?' said Andrieu. 'That's all they were afraid of – someone finding out that they'd taken the car for a spin?'

'It's not such a trivial thing; they could have got the sack.

Staff aren't supposed to go joy-riding in guests' cars. But the main thing was, when we heard about what happened afterwards, Jeanne was afraid that Gilbert might have done some damage to the car, with driving too fast and not being familiar with the controls – she said he crashed the gears at high speed, at one point, and it made the most horrible noise. And once he had to really slam the brakes on, because he wasn't used to driving at that kind of speed and he underestimated how long it would take to stop. She was worried that it might have been something like that that caused the accident. And they were both afraid that someone might have noticed there were more kilometres on the clock than there should have been. We thought that was why you were nosing round, asking questions.'

'No, not exactly,' said Andrieu.

'Why were you asking questions, then?'

'It doesn't matter now.'

22

Now, in the early morning queue at Madame P's, Zoe found herself watching her fellow shoppers with new eyes. She was becoming suspicious of everyone. It was a most unpleasant sensation.

The taller of the two young Englishmen joined the queue behind her.

'Any more news about your car?' she said. The paint-spraying had been reported to the local gendarme, who was supposed to be making enquiries.

The young man said: 'No, not really. At first, we assumed it was the usual.'

'What do you mean?'

'Homophobia. Happens all the time. Then we thought, maybe it had something to do with the *pétanque* match – we got to the semi-final, remember? Some of the locals weren't too pleased about that.'

'Injured pride? Seems a bit extreme.'

'Well, not so much pride as money. We upset the odds on the betting. I've heard that one or two people lost quite a bit of money.'

'What does the gendarme have to say about that?'

'He thinks it's just vandalism, probably a bunch of local tearaways. Apparently, some people saw a gang of youths on motor bikes, hanging round the car-park earlier in the evening. The gendarme thinks they may have done it. It wouldn't have been directed at us specifically – they'd just have gone for a foreign car, because if they picked a local one the owner might find out who was responsible and come round and give them a thrashing. Foreigners are safer – here today, gone tomorrow.'

Yes, but why these particular foreigners? Zoe wondered, pedalling back towards the villa, as the young man's paint-spattered Volvo overtook her. The restaurant that night had been full of foreigners: Germans, Belgians, Dutch; even other English. Their cars were in the car-park, too. Why were they unscathed?

Because, she suddenly realized, watching the car disappear into the distance, they weren't Volvos.

Andrieu was depressed. His St-Flour initiative had come to nothing. It did now appear, from a few further enquiries, that the hotel receptionist had told the truth; the whole incident had been nothing more than a joy-ride. Which not only wiped out the only potential candidate for the car-tampering exercise, but also made it even more difficult to see when or how anyone else could have got at the vehicle.

On top of that, when he got home, he had phoned Martine and there had been no reply. He had only himself to blame. Diverted by the confusions of the case – and, he had to admit, by recurrent images of Joelle Rocard – he hadn't called her for days; she probably thought he'd lost interest. Serve him right for lusting after married women. Unable to sleep, he'd come to work early, and sat at his desk, hoping for inspiration; but none was forthcoming.

'Message for you from Zoe Chavanac,' he said, when Albuisson turned up at a civilized hour. 'Something about a Volvo.'

'Anything else?'

He reported the essence of the hotel receptionist's statement.

Albuisson sighed. 'There goes another duck,' he said, cryptically. 'Get on to the newspaper office, will you, see if they've come up with anything yet. I'll phone Zoe.'

'Two things,' said Andrieu. 'First of all, the newspaper people have found the letter placing the order for the latest ad. This is the copy they faxed; they're sending the original.'

Albuisson squinted at the fax. It looked much like the previous letter they had seen – same typeface, same layout. The text of the message was different, of course, and the name; and this time the address was in St-Rémy de Provence.

'A false address, naturally,' said Andrieu.

'And a false name,' said Albuisson; even he'd heard of C. Monet. 'It was the same arrangement, I take it – no postmark, payment in cash?'

'Yes, but here comes the second thing: someone remembered it arriving. It was delivered by motor bike messenger. Unfortunately, they didn't notice the name of the delivery company.'

'Motor bike?' said Albuisson, brightening. His smile faded. 'No. It doesn't make sense.'

'What doesn't?'

He said: 'Zoe Chavanac thinks she knows what the incident was that triggered this advertisement. Last Friday night, an English-registered car, a Volvo, was vandalized, sprayed with paint, right outside the restaurant where she and Claude were having dinner. They'd been driven there by her brother . . .'

'Don't tell me,' said Andrieu. 'He's English and he drives a Volvo.'

'Exactly. Zoe thinks that someone must have seen them leave the villa and followed them to see where they were going – but probably not all the way to the restaurant. It's in a very small village; if this person had followed all the way, he'd have risked being seen – and there was no need to take the risk, because there's virtually nothing there except this one restaurant. So if the Chavanacs were going to that village, it was a safe bet they were going to that restaurant.

'But, because this person didn't follow them the whole way, he wouldn't have known that Zoe's brother had dropped her and Claude at the restaurant, driven out the other side of the village, and gone back to the villa. He must have assumed that all three of them had gone into the restaurant, and left the car in the car-park. He probably waited until all the customers had parked and gone into the restaurant, and there was no one else around. And then he went along to the car-park and, sure enough, there was an English-registered Volvo. A different registration number, of course, and not quite the same colour, but he probably wouldn't have noticed – it would have been getting dark by then.'

'So he vandalized the wrong car.'

'Can't say for certain, but it's possible. And what's interesting is that someone reported a gang of youths hanging round the car-park – on motor bikes.'

'Motor bikes, motor bikes,' Andrieu said. 'Are you saying this might have been the Louisots? They hardly amount to a gang of youths, do they?'

'You know how witnesses exaggerate, especially about things like this. Three people having an altercation in the street becomes a riot. Two kids on a motor bike can easily become a gang – and if they're both wearing helmets and leathers, it's hard to tell who they are, or if they're male or female.' Albuisson toyed with the fax. 'I presume you've still got the number of Louisot's flat-mate?'

Andrieu nodded.

'Give him a call. Ask him if Louisot's interested in art.'

Andrieu went off to his desk. He was back five minutes later.

'He reckons Gregoire wouldn't know a Picasso from a Peugeot. But the girl would. He doesn't know much about her, but he does know one thing: she's an art student.'

'Who was that?' said Hugo, as Claude replaced the handset on the phone. 'The laughing policeman?'

'Don't be cruel,' said Zoe. 'Georges may be a little gloomy, but he has his moments.'

'He wanted to know if the name Louisot rang a bell,' said Claude.

'Louisot?'

'That's what the Newlyweds are called, apparently. Gregoire and Laurence Louisot.'

'That's it!' said Moira.

'What?'

'When there was someone out in the orchard, remember? I said I heard a name, but I couldn't for the life of me think what it was? Well, that was it: Laurence.'

'But you said it was a man's name that you heard,' protested Claude.

Moira looked puzzled. 'It is – Laurence Olivier, Laurence Harvey, Larry the Lamb . . .'

'. . . Yves St Laurent,' said Zoe. 'Moira, in France, Laurence is a girl's name. If it's a boy, it's Laurent.'

'Oh,' said Moira, slowly. She looked at Claude. 'Well, did this name, Louisot, mean anything to you?'

'Not in the slightest,' he said.

Suppose, thought Albuisson, just suppose for one moment that it might be Louisot. Disregard the alibis. Disregard the fact that Chavanac didn't know him, had never even heard of him. What was left?

Proximity to the Chavanacs: Louisot had been at their villa several times, socially – and could easily have been there at other times, too. Then there was the motor bike; and he knew about engines. The girl was an art student: she could have given him the idea for the false names, or perhaps he'd just taken them from one of her art books.

What about access to a computer and printer? That might not be so significant after all. Maria Zwitalska had given him the clue: the first three ads were created individually, after the events they referred to. But the later ones could have been produced at any time – a batch of them prepared in advance, undated, suitable for whatever might arise.

Zwitalska's analysis had also pointed to confusion, uncertainty, recklessness . . . signs of youth and immaturity? But youth also argued against Louisot; a decade ago, he would – according to the date of birth on his vehicle registration documents – have been just nine years old. Unless, of course, that 'ten years' ad was a false trail, deliberately laid.

What was known about Louisot? Not much. Was that in itself significant? If he was just an innocent holidaymaker, wouldn't the people around know more about him? No, maybe not. Everyone expects honeymooners to be wrapped up in themselves.

A country boy, anyway; that much they knew. Albuisson prowled across the office to the map of France pinned to the wall. Somewhere near Confolens, Andrieu had said. He pinpointed the area: Limoges to the east, the nearest big town, but still some distance away; Périgueux to the south, Angoulême south-west, Poitiers north-west. The middle of nowhere.

A whirlwind romance with a girl from the past – had they been childhood sweethearts? Had they grown up together out there in the sticks, and then her family moved away to the big city? Who was she, and did she know what was going on?

Too many questions; stick to facts. Louisot had a brother, and a father sufficiently well-off and indulgent to pay for an expensive motor bike in cash. He studied engineering – what was it Andrieu had said? Stress tolerance. Breaking point.

He felt well on the way to that right now.

They were becalmed, uncertain what move to make next. Andrieu was reading a newspaper. Albuisson retired to his office and made coffee, slowly and meticulously: ground the carefully chosen beans – not too fine, not too coarse – and tipped them into the *cafetière*; poured the freshly boiling water over them; put the filter and the lid in place, and waited.

Then he heard a whoop like a cowboy's: 'Yee-hoo!'

He looked round and saw Andrieu coming through the door, waving the newspaper in the air.

'What's the matter with you?'

'Look at this.'

Andrieu spread the paper on the desk, open at the second page. Albuisson scanned it. He could see nothing of significance. A road accident report, a house fire, a dog that had saved its owner from drowning, a local dignitary visiting Japan, a couple of adverts.

'There!' said Andrieu, jabbing his finger impatiently at a quarter-page ad in the bottom left-hand corner. 'I could kick myself. This ad's been in the paper every day this week, and I've only just noticed it.'

It was something about a car, a particular model, that owners should take to their dealer for checks; there was a line drawing of the vehicle. It meant nothing to Albuisson.

'It's a product recall,' said Andrieu. 'A fault in the 5600i special edition, cars that were made between April and December last year. The manufacturers have found that some of them may have a problem with a valve in the brake hydraulics, that causes a sudden loss of – '

'Could you start again,' said Albuisson, 'only this time in plain French?'

'Some of these cars', said Andrieu, 'have duff brakes.'

'Yes?'

'Well, it's the 5600i special edition – don't you recognize it? That's what Claude Chavanac was driving. And I'll bet, if we check the engine number, we'll find that his car was one of this batch. Do you see what I'm getting at? Nobody needed to fix the brakes; they failed of their own accord.'

'We could have Louisot brought in,' said Andrieu.

'What are we going to charge him with? Failing to cause a car crash? Being on holiday in Provence? Owning a motor bike? Being in possession of a more attractive wife than he deserves?'

'We don't have to charge him. Just get him in for questioning.'

'We still have to have a good reason,' said Albuisson. 'And even if his alibi for the car crash is irrelevant now, don't forget he still has an alibi for the falling rock incident. If there was just one thing, one single thing, to link him to Claude Chavanac, then . . .'

He stopped.

'What?' said Andrieu.

'Just a minute.'

Albuisson sifted through papers on his desk; found what he was looking for, dialled a phone number, waited.

'Madame Jouvet?' Andrieu heard him say. 'Georges Albuisson, St-Geraud police . . . yes, thank you . . . no, just a quick question. Your old friend, Marie-Christine: you told me that when she divorced her husband she reverted to her maiden name. You couldn't tell me what that name was, could you? Yes? And the children: did they take that name, too? Ah. Thank you.'

He hung up, and turned to Andrieu.

'That phone number you called, registered to Bernard Louisot – that's not Gregoire's father; it's his grandfather. Marie-Christine Brasseur's maiden name was Louisot, and Bernard is her father. Gregoire Louisot is Jean-Michel Artaud's son.'

23

'They've got him!' Andrieu mouthed across the office, jabbing his thumb in the air. He listened for a few minutes longer, saying, 'Yes . . . yes . . . fine . . . we'll get back to you,' and then put down the phone.

'Traffic cops picked up Gregoire Louisot in the early hours of this morning,' he told Albuisson. 'Eastbound on the A8, heading for Italy – he almost made it, too. He was clocking over 200 kilometres an hour when they spotted him. They kept him in custody overnight; they're taking him back to Apt this morning.'

'What about the girl?'

'Don't know. She wasn't with him. She wasn't at the house they were renting, either. They're on the look-out for her.'

'I'd better get down there,' said Albuisson.

'You want me to come with you?' offered Andrieu, hopefully.

'No, you stay here; there may be things that need to be done at this end. And someone has to feed that wretched cat.'

He took the train. A police car met him at Avignon station; he went to the Chavanacs' villa first, to tell them what was happening, and then to the village to inspect the house where the Louisots had been living.

A policeman was guarding the door, fending off unwanted attention from inquisitive spectators. The house was at the top of the village, old and narrow; three floors – the kitchen at the bottom, and above that the *salon*, with a big open fireplace; at the top there was a bedroom, shower-room and toilet, and a door that led to a roof-terrace. Light slanted in at awkward angles through half-shuttered windows. The bed was unmade.

'They've left a few clothes; there's some food in the kitchen, and soap and things in the bathroom,' the policeman said. 'But the owner's had a look round, and she says everything else belongs here.'

Albuisson was disappointed. He'd been hoping for more than that – papers, books, anything. He went around opening cupboards and pulling out drawers, but found only the impersonal, practical necessities of a house that had been furnished for brief occupation by strangers.

Except: there was ash in the fireplace.

Who would light a fire in this weather?

Albuisson crouched by the hearth and fingered the little pile of ash. It was cold, but he was sure it was recent; too neat and undisturbed to have been there since the winter. It was soft and flaky. Burnt paper, he thought. Too well-burnt, probably, to give up many secrets, even to forensics' finest; but at least it was something.

Also in the fireplace, he noticed, was a little litter of discarded pistachio shells.

The police car took him to Apt.

'He's in there,' said the station officer.

Albuisson peered through the small glass panel in the door. Watched over by a bored policeman, Gregoire Louisot sat behind a table in a hot, bare interview room, looking very young and tired. On the table, in a clear plastic bag, were the personal possessions taken from him after his arrest. His leather jacket, gauntlets and motor cycle helmet lay on a chair in the corner of the room.

'Has he said anything?' Albuisson asked.

'Not yet.'

'What's he been charged with?'

'Speeding, dangerous driving, possession of illegal substances.'

'Oh?'

'In his jacket – some pills and a tab of acid. The traffic boys said he was either drunk or high when they stopped him, but we don't have the results of the blood tests yet.'

'Anything else of interest?'

'No. Want to talk to him now?'

Albuisson nodded.

There are certain materials used to build recording studios, so that all the sound is absorbed by the walls and nothing reflected back, and that's what the interview room felt like to Albuisson. Gregoire Louisot sat impassively, absorbing his questions; not uncooperative, exactly – he was placid and polite, uncomplaining, no hysterical demands to see his lawyer – but nor was he going out of his way to assist the police in their enquiries.

'Your father's name was Jean-Michel Artaud, wasn't it?' Albuisson said.

'Yes.'

'He was imprisoned for fraud when you were nine years old.'

'Yes.'

'Your mother divorced him and you went to live with your grandparents, until you left to go to college in Paris.'

'Yes.'

'Your father died earlier this year, and left you quite a lot of money. You spent some of it on a motor bike.'

'Yes.'

'Did you love your father, Gregoire?'

'I d-don't know.'

'When did you last see him?'

'I don't know.'

'Oh, I think you do. When he died, the police found your Paris address in his wallet. They called you to identify his body. Your mother had kept him away from you, but he renewed contact with you when you moved to Paris, didn't he?'

Grudgingly: 'Yes.'

'And you saw him several times after that.'

'N-now and then.'

'How did you feel about him?'

'I don't know.'

This could go on all day, thought Albuisson. He cast around

for inspiration. Through the clear plastic of the bag on the table, he could see Louisot's personal possessions. Nothing out of the ordinary: a wallet, handkerchief, cigarettes and lighter, chewing gum, keys, a pair of mini-binoculars, a comb, some small change . . . wait a minute.

He opened the bag and took out the cigarette lighter, inspected it, stood it on the table between himself and Louisot. It was red plastic, disposable.

His voice and his expression hardened; no more Mister Nice Guy. He said: 'Let's get to the point. We found a lighter like this in Claude Chavanac's garden, near where you started the woodpile fire. Your fingerprints are on it. And we've got the letters you sent to the newspapers. It's amazing what we can do with forensics nowadays; I think we'll find those letters match up with the ash in the grate at the house where you've been living. That's where you burnt the remaining letters, isn't it? The ones you hadn't used yet. The ash is being analysed now.'

'I've n-no idea what you m-m-mean.' The boy's voice was still flat, but there was a flicker of anxiety now; the stammer was more pronounced. Albuisson knew he'd triggered something. He decided to go for broke.

'Then let me explain,' he said. 'Your father was charged with fraud and embezzlement. Claude Chavanac was his lawyer. He lost the case and your father went to prison. That changed your whole life, didn't it? You were uprooted, moved away from Paris, made to grow up without a father. Your mother became angry and bitter; she tried to turn you against your father – but you still loved him, didn't you? You resented the way he'd been taken away from you. When you met up again in Paris, it brought it home to you just what you'd been missing all these years.

'Then, just as you were getting to know your father again, he was killed in an accident. I'll bet you were pretty upset. I'll bet you were really angry about what had happened to your life. And when you're angry, you want to get even; you look around for someone to blame.

'You hit on Claude Chavanac, didn't you? Why was that? Had your father told you he was innocent, was that it? That he shouldn't have gone to prison, that his lawyer should have got him off? Or did you just make that up in your own head? Either way, you'd found yourself someone to put the blame on.

'And you had something else, too, that you didn't have before: you had money. Enough to buy a big, fast motor bike – so you could cover long distances quickly. Enough to rent a house in Provence for a month at high-season prices. Enough to go wherever you wanted without having to think twice about the cost.

'You hadn't really thought out what you were going to do; you just wanted to lash out at Chavanac in some way – and when you read in the papers that he'd been in a car crash, that's what gave you the idea, isn't it? You went down to St-Geraud, found out where he lived, where he worked; and you placed an ad in the local paper, to scare him – to make him think that the car crash wasn't an accident, that someone was trying to kill him.

'You couldn't do much more than that at the time, because he was in hospital and you couldn't get at him there. So you waited till he came out, and then you went back to St-Geraud. It only takes a few hours from Paris these days, doesn't it, down the A71 on that new motor bike of yours? You could get there and back whenever you wanted to, no trouble.

'You set fire to the logpile. You could have burnt down the whole house, you know, with Chavanac's wife and children inside. Was that what you wanted? I don't think you really knew what you wanted, did you? You just did the first thing that came into your head. You broke into his apartment and destroyed his books – how did you know about the books? Did your father tell you? I expect he would have known; he and Chavanac were friends at one time, weren't they?

'And, in each case, you put an ad in the papers – but not right away; it was always a few days afterwards. Now, why was that? Could it be because the first one hadn't appeared until a few days after the car crash, and you wanted to make the others look like part of the same pattern – to add to the evidence that the car crash was caused deliberately? That's what you wanted Chavanac to think, wasn't it? That his life really was in danger.

'Unfortunately, it all fell a bit flat, because he didn't notice the ads. So you sent copies to his office – but even then, he didn't get the message. He put the papers on one side and went on holiday.

'You followed him. Found a place to rent nearby, and carried on with your little tricks. In Paris, you had access to a computer – at your college, was it? – and you'd been using that to write your letters to the papers. But you couldn't do that in Provence, so you made up some letters in advance, and took them with you.

'It was easy to get close to Chavanac. You even went to his house as a guest – you felt quite safe, because he didn't know who you were. You knew he wouldn't recognize you – he hadn't seen you since you were a child; and you weren't known by your father's name.

'You pulled off some nasty little pranks: cancelling a restaurant reservation, drowning a cat, spraying paint on a car – you do know it was the wrong car, I suppose?

'But you also did something very dangerous: you dropped a rock off the roof on to the chair where you expected Chavanac to be sitting. He was lucky – he wasn't there when it fell. If he had been, it would probably have killed him. I intend to charge you with attempted murder.'

For the first time, Louisot interrupted. There was an edge of panic in his voice now. 'You c-c-can't do that! I was at the F-f-fontaine de Vaucluse that day. Ask Chavanac's wife – she saw me there, I know she did. I was there when it happened.'

Albuisson said, quietly; 'How do you know when it happened?'

'But, hang on,' said Andrieu, as the centime finally dropped. 'That lighter you found in the garden hasn't even come back from the lab yet.'

'I know that,' said Albuisson. 'But Louisot doesn't.'

'That's misleading a suspect. Lawyers take a dim view of that sort of thing.' And so did Albuisson, normally; this case must be really getting to him.

'I don't think it matters now. He's made a voluntary statement, no pressure. We gave him a break, something to eat and drink, and then he started talking and it all came tumbling out. How his whole life had been blighted by his father's imprisonment. How he was forced to leave Paris and all his friends, and go live in the back of beyond. How his mother was angry and bad-tempered all the time, and his grandparents were strict and old-fashioned, and he never had any fun.

'He figured that the only way out was to do well at school, pass his exams, and get a place at college – which he did. He went to Paris, met up with his father again, and the rest was just as I'd suggested.'

'But what *did* happen with the falling rock?'

'Ah, now; that was clever. He used his engineering skills. He'd been studying stress tolerance of materials under different conditions. One of the materials he'd been working with was wood that had been treated in some particular way – don't ask me the details; I didn't understand the technicalities. Whatever it is, though, it makes the wood very flexible – but only up to a certain temperature; above that, it reverts to its normal state. He'd taken a piece of this wood with him to Provence – he didn't have any particular plan for it; he was just intrigued by its properties, and thought it might come in useful.

'What he did was to get up on the roof of the Chavanacs' villa. He'd been there, with a load of other people, at a drinks party, which gave him the chance to reconnoitre the place without anybody getting suspicious – that's when he discovered how to get into the roof-space. It was a perfect place to hide, and to eavesdrop on conversations down below. That's how he knew that Chavanac was going to be alone in the house while everyone else was at the Fontaine de Vaucluse.

'He'd also been watching the villa with binoculars from his roof-terrace up in the village, so he knew that Chavanac regularly used to sit in this particular spot on the north side of the house during the heat of the day, and he didn't move about much because of his bad leg.

'So, after dark, Louisot climbed out on the roof and set up a slab of rock supported by his special piece of wood, so that the wood was under stress but not breaking. And since it was on the northern side of the house, it stayed relatively cool until well into the next day. Eventually, though, when the sun got high enough, the wood heated up; it snapped, and the rock fell. But by this time, Louisot and his wife were at the Fontaine de Vaucluse, making sure that they were seen by the Chavanac party. And afterwards, nobody saw anything suspicious in a broken piece of wood among the debris.'

Andrieu was impressed. 'He's obviously smarter than he looks,' he said.

'So it would seem.'

'What about the girl? Where does she come into it?'

'He insists she wasn't part of it. She knew what he was up to, didn't approve, but couldn't persuade him to stop. She didn't realize how serious it was; she thought it was just practical jokes.'

'Dropping a rock on someone's head isn't much of a joke.'

'He maintains that she never knew what he'd done. He told her it was just a small stone, that it wouldn't do any real damage.'

'She must be pretty stupid.'

'Or in love. It's amazing what people will believe when they're in love.'

'Where is she now?'

'He doesn't know – or won't say. He realized we were on to him yesterday; he was up in the roof again, planning some new piece of mischief, when I phoned Chavanac to ask if the name Louisot meant anything to him. He heard Chavanac telling the others what I'd said.'

'So that's why he scarpered.'

'He suggested to the girl that they should split up. He thought – rightly – that we'd be looking for him and the motor bike, and she'd be safer on her own. He's very protective; he'll talk about himself, but not her. He won't give anything away – her maiden name, where her family is, which college she goes to, anything that might tell us where she'd go.'

'But how far could she get without transport?'

'He may have dropped her at a railway station, in which case she could be anywhere by now. We've got someone watching the house where they were staying, in case she tries to go back there, and also Louisot's apartment in Paris, and his grand-parents' farm. We've also got someone tracing records; if we can find their marriage certificate, that'll tell us who she is. He refuses to say where or when they were married, so it might take some time – but we'll find her, in the end.'

'So that's it, then,' said Andrieu. 'Over, finished.' He felt cheated, not being in on the kill. 'What are you going to do now?'

'I'm invited to the Chavanacs' villa for dinner.'

'Oh, very nice,' said Andrieu, sniffily. *'Bon appétit.'*

'Which reminds me: don't forget to feed the cat.'

24

There was a sense of things coming to an end. It was the last weekend of August, and the *rentrée* was beginning, the long trail home from the holidays. The radio was broadcasting the usual tales of traffic jams and motorway pile-ups. In Provence, the season would linger on for several weeks yet; the sun would go on shining, the grapes would go on ripening, there would still be visitors crowding the tourist attractions; but the high-summer hysteria was over.

Albuisson was experiencing a similar sensation. The enquiry was far from complete; there were formal statements to be taken, evidence to be collected, legal procedures to be followed. But in practical terms, it was all over bar the shouting. He felt a mixture of satisfaction and disappointment; it was always somehow disappointing when a case like this came to an end. The conclusion should have been neater, cleverer, more dramatic. But the truth was generally banal and rather sad; extraordinary acts committed by ordinary people for the most mundane reasons.

He had been happy to accept the Chavanacs' hospitality overnight. Their relief that the ordeal was over had turned the evening into quite a celebration, and a great deal of wine had been consumed – as his head reminded him, to his regret, when he woke in the morning. He went down to breakfast to find other members of the party subdued over their croissants, with the radio playing very quietly indeed.

Moira came in looking half asleep. 'Has anyone seen Chiara?' she said.

'I saw her earlier, playing outside,' said Lucie. 'Near the *pétanque* pitch.'

Moira went out again. Zoe said: 'Anyone want more coffee?' Several people yawned.

Moira came back. 'I still can't find her,' she said.

Hugo, heavy-eyed, got up reluctantly. 'I'll go and look for her,' he said. 'She can't have gone far; she's only got little legs.'

It was about half an hour before the reality sunk in. This wasn't a joke. Chiara really was missing.

'It's the girl,' said Albuisson, grimly. 'It must be.'

'What girl?' Hugo wasn't thinking straight.

'Louisot's wife, Laurence. She must be still in the area somewhere.'

'But why? Why would she take Chiara?'

'As a hostage,' said Moira, bluntly. They had all expected her to go to pieces, but adversity had brought out the old Moira, unsentimental and businesslike, making lists and organizing things. She said: 'The girl is presumably trying to protect her husband. She must think she can somehow persuade the police to release him in exchange for Chiara.'

'If that's so, then wouldn't she have contacted someone by now?'

'Not necessarily. She'd need to get out of reach first, and find a safe hiding-place.'

'But why Chiara?' said Claude.'I'm the one Louisot was after; she must know that Chiara's not my daughter.'

'I doubt if that would matter now,' said Albuisson. 'If Moira's right – and I think she probably is – this isn't directed against you; it's just a desperate act by a desperate girl. She took Chiara because that was all she could do. Your own children are too big and too aware of what's happening.'

'We let our defences down too soon,' said Zoe, miserably. 'We'd been so bloody careful, ever since we knew that someone was trying to get at us; we never let any of the kids out of our sight.'

'It's not your fault,' said Albuisson. 'I should have known. I just never thought of anything like this. I'd assumed the girl would just run; get as far away as possible. But that's the problem, you see: we don't know anything about her. We don't know *what* she's likely to do. We need to know what makes her tick.'

'Isn't there anything?' said Zoe. 'Anything at all that we know about her?'

Albuisson said: 'We know she hasn't been with Louisot very long – but they'd known each other before, although we don't know where or how. We know she's an art student in Paris, quite a streetwise young lady by the sound of it. We know that Louisot is crazy about her. And that's about it, I'm afraid.'

'No, it's not,' said Moira. 'We also know that she had a young sister who drowned as a child – and because of that she's got a thing about water.' Her brisk demeanour suddenly crumpled. 'Though what help that is to us, I don't know. God, it's hopeless.'

Zoe put her arms around her. 'We'll find Chiara, don't worry.'

'She's so *little*,' sobbed Moira. 'Please God, let her be all right.'

Andrieu was taken aback to get a phone call from Albuisson at home on a Sunday morning; his first thought was that his boss was checking up on him to make sure he'd fed that damn cat. He listened as Albuisson told him of the child's disappearance.

'What do you want me to do?' he said. 'Should I go in to HQ?'

'No, there's nothing you can do – except *think*. Think if there's any way, any way at all, that we can find out more about this girl.'

'Presumably you've already tried Louisot's family – his mother, his brother, his grandparents? Don't they know anything about her?'

'They've never heard of her. None of them had seen him for months. He hadn't told anyone that he was married; they didn't even know he had a girlfriend. His flat-mate in Paris couldn't tell us any more than he'd already told us – doesn't know her surname, doesn't know any of her friends. She wasn't part of their usual crowd. He doesn't even know which college she goes to.'

'Then I'm sorry, but I'm out of ideas.'

'Well, keep thinking. And if you do think of anything, call

me straight away at the Chavanacs' villa. If you don't get an answer there, try the local gendarmerie; that's where the search is being co-ordinated.'

He read out a number; Andrieu wrote it down, saying: 'Incidentally, I know you've got more important things on your mind, but this might cheer you up. There's a small piece in the paper here this morning about Denis Brunet. It looks like the shit's about to hit the fan. I just thought you might like to know.'

Denis Brunet. As he heard the name, the voice of his mother, of all people, suddenly floated unbidden into Albuisson's mind. Odd, she was saying, to call the daughter after the father and the son after the mother.

Odd, perhaps – but maybe not unique?

'I think,' he told a bewildered Andrieu, 'you may have just given me the answer.'

He put down the phone and turned to Claude. 'The Grissot case defendants were old friends of yours, weren't they? You knew their families?'

'Yes.'

'What were the names of the Jouvet children?'

Claude frowned, scouring his memory. 'There were three of them,' he said, 'a boy and two girls. The little girl was called Nicole, I think, and the boy was Daniel, and the other girl, the eldest . . . oh, God; I see what you mean. They called her after her father. Her name was Laurence.'

The villa was horribly quiet. Everyone else – along with the local police and gendarmerie and half the population of the neighbourhood – was out scouring the countryside. Even Fredy and Lucie were with them; they didn't want to be left out, and despite the risks it seemed better to make them feel useful than to leave them moping.

Only Claude was left behind. Someone had to stay at the villa in case . . . well, in case of what, he didn't like to dwell on too closely; but, being incapacitated, he was the obvious candidate.

The tension was unbearable, just waiting. Claude was no good at waiting, at leaving the action to others. He cursed his immobility; he couldn't even pace the floor. He limped to the kitchen in search of something to eat, and looked longingly at the bottles in the wine rack. No, he told himself; keep a clear head.

He heard a voice: 'Hello? Hello, is there anybody there?', and a face appeared round the kitchen door. 'Ah, there you are.' It was the Municipal Maintenance Department. 'I gather you've lost a little girl,' he said.

'Yes?' said Claude.

'I didn't know anything about it, you see, because I'd been out to my sister's. But then when I got back just now, the wife said they were all out looking for this kiddy, and I thought, well, I'd better go straight round there and tell them.'

'Tell them what?'

'It was this morning, late-ish. I'm off to my sister's, in the van, and there's this young woman and a little girl, walking along the side of the road, not far from here. Well, I recognized them both, of course, because I'd seen them before . . .'

'You recognized the little girl? It was definitely Chiara?'

'I don't know what she's called, but I know I've seen her here. A little blue dress, she had on. And the other one, she's been staying up in the village – that young couple with the motor bike, you know?'

Claude felt his pulse begin to race. 'What happened?'

'Well, she waves me down and says where am I going, and I say Fontaine de Vaucluse – because that's where my sister lives; well, just outside, actually – and she says can I give them a lift. She says she's taking the little girl out for the day. And I thought, well, maybe she's got some arrangement, you know, babysitting or whatever. And the little girl seemed quite happy with her; she was holding her hand and trotting along, not upset or anything. So I gave them a ride.'

'Did this young woman say anything on the way?'

'No, she wasn't very chatty. But some people aren't, are they? The kiddy was quiet, too – but, like I said, she didn't seem upset. I dropped them off just outside the centre, and went on to my sister's. Last I saw of them, they were walking down the final bit of road into the town.' The man paused, frowning. 'What did you say the little girl was called?'

'Chiara.'

'Funny, that. It was definitely her, I know it was – but I'm sure I heard that young woman calling her Nicky.'

There was only an answerphone at the gendarmerie; everyone was out searching. Claude dictated a message, but he couldn't leave it at that. He had to do something. What? He had no transport: Zoe had taken their car, Hugo and Moira the Volvo. He turned to the hapless Municipal Maintenance Department.

'Wait there, while I get my crutches,' he said.

It was Sunday afternoon. The queues of traffic heading for the Fontaine de Vaucluse trailed back almost to the town of l'Isle-sur-la-Sorgue, seven kilometres away.

'They're all queueing to get into the car-parks,' said Claude. 'Just overtake, for Christ's sake.'

'I can't see whether there's anything coming,' protested the Municipal Maintenance Department.

'Of course there's nothing coming,' cried Claude, impatiently. 'On Sunday afternoons, everyone is trying to get *in*to Fontaine de Vaucluse. No one is coming out. That's why there's a traffic jam.'

'If you say so,' said the Municipal Maintenance Department, pulling out on a bend and narrowly avoiding an oncoming laundry van.

It seemed utterly hopeless. The crowds were so dense; solid flows of people pushing relentlessly in all directions, like lava. Old people, moving slowly; children, rushing and dashing and tripping. People walking five or six abreast, people walking backwards and sideways and not looking where they were going. Cameras. Videos. Ice creams. Dogs.

The broad promenade along the bank of the river narrowed into a well-worn path of rock and earth – far from ideal for a man on crutches. Claude stumbled along as best he could, cursing when he slipped on the smooth rock or jarred his foot on the uneven surface. And after all this, there was no guarantee that Chiara and the girl would be here.

But they were.

He saw the flash of blue first, Chiara's dress, through a gap in the crowd; then people moved, and it was gone. He pushed through roughly, wielding the crutches like weapons, people staring back at him, affronted.

Now he could see them. They were close to the water's edge, at the brink of the cavern. The girl was sitting on the ground, hugging Chiara, rocking slowly back and forth. Chiara was chuckling; she thought it was a game.

His self-confidence, normally unassailable, evaporated. He had no idea what to do.

But he must do something. He moved forward as cautiously as he could, but sneaking up on someone is no easy matter for a man on crutches. The girl looked up and saw him.

He froze, terrified of precipitating any sudden movement so near to the water. But she didn't move. Regaining confidence, he went closer. He even ventured a smile.

'Hello, Laurence,' he said, gently.

She almost spat: 'Bastard!'

So; it was going to be difficult. He said, as calmly as he could: 'Look, I'm sorry about Gregoire. I know he's had a hard time. But this isn't going to help him, you know.'

'Oh, fuck Gregoire!' she said.

She spoke with a coarse Parisian accent, so exaggerated that he knew it must be false; an unconvincing ersatz toughness, like a nun trying to talk dirty.

He said: 'I know you're just trying to protect him – and he's trying to protect you.'

'Yes, well, he would, the stupid prick.'

There was something very wrong here, but he couldn't get the measure of it. He assessed the chances of simply making a grab for Chiara, but he knew it wouldn't work; he couldn't do it while holding the crutches, and without them he couldn't move fast enough.

He tried again, in the soft, reassuring voice that had always worked so well with anxious clients and hesitant women. 'Gregoire has told the police what happened – there's no need for you to be afraid; he told them it had nothing to do with you.'

A scornful little smile spread across the girl's face. 'What did he tell them?' she said. 'That he did it because of his dad? Because you got his dad put away and he hated you for it?'

'That's what he said.'

She sneered at him. 'He hated his fucking father.'

Now he was utterly confused. He said: 'What was it all about, then?'

'You don't think he'd have had the nous to do all that stuff, do you? He couldn't find his arse with both hands without a map. I don't suppose he even thought up his own confession, did he? I expect some cleverdick policeman put the words into his mouth, and he said yes, right, it was me, it's a fair cop. He'd do that; he's like fucking plasticine. "Go buy a bike, Gregoire." "Right, then." "Let's get married, Gregoire." "Right, then." He's so desperate to please, it's pitiful. Do you really think he'd have the imagination to think up all that stuff we did? Even that bit of bloody wood was my idea. He had the equipment, but he didn't have a clue what to do with it.' She sniffed. 'In more ways that one – not that *that* bothered me much.'

'So it was all your idea?' said Claude, softly.

'Yes,' she said. 'He was useful; I convinced him that he ought to hate you – even if he didn't. And he had money. And he'd do anything I wanted. But it was my idea.'

'Why, Laurence? Why?'

'You were my dad's lawyer, too.'

'But he was acquitted.'

'He was guilty, though, wasn't he?'

'The court didn't think so.'

'No – because you bloody defended him. Came out with all your smooth talk and your rotten lawyer's lies, so they let him off instead of putting him where he belonged. Then at least we might have had some peace. We might have got away from him. She might have understood.'

'Who might have understood?'

'My mum, who d'you think? She might have opened her eyes and seen what he was like.'

'What was he like, Laurence?'

'Like you, that's what. You're all the bloody same. You think you were put on this earth to screw, and we were put here to lie back and let you do it. The only difference is, I don't suppose you're into little girls.'

'Oh, God,' said Claude, finally understanding.

'He's fucking useless, as well. I used to pray my little heart out every night: don't let my dad come near me, let my mum come in and catch him at it, let him crash his car on the way home. Fat lot of good that did me.'

Claude said: 'Laurence, this may be my fault; it may be your father's fault. But it certainly isn't Chiara's fault. Let her go.'

She looked down at Chiara as though she had forgotten she was there.

'What, so the same thing can happen to her?'

'Nothing will happen to her.'

'That's what everybody says. But it will! Why will no one ever listen to me? Once she's a bit older, he'll start on her as well. She'll have to go through it all, just like I did.'

Her voice was quite different now; she had regressed into a well-brought-up little *bourgeoise*. She looked at Claude with downright hatred, and he realized it wasn't him that she was seeing.

'I won't let it happen,' she said. 'I won't let you have her.' She grabbed Chiara, pulling her closer. 'It's all right,' she whispered to her. 'Don't worry, Nicky, it's all right.'

She stood up and moved closer to the water's edge. One step, accidental or deliberate; that was all it would take. Behind her, the river surged out from the rock, swollen by last week's rains; and beyond that, the cavern was dark and fathomless.

Claude looked around in despair, alone in the crowd. There were hundreds of people, coming and going, taking photographs, taking no notice. What did they think they were seeing? A family row? In a sense – in the girl's confused mind – they were right; except that he was not her father, and Chiara not her sister.

He could try to enlist someone's help, but how long would it take to explain what was happening? Would anyone believe him? And above all, there was the risk that the girl would be panicked by some clumsy attempt to help. By default, he edged nearer to the water, matching the girls' step for step, though it was dangerous; he was in no fit state for tricky manoeuvres.

'Don't you come near us,' she hissed.

But now he had got himself into a position from which he could, if he was quick enough, place himself between her and the water. He waited, choosing his moment; a dog came along, friendly, wagging its tail, and Chiara reached out to it, distracting the girl. Claude made his move, struggling to keep his balance, fiercely shoving the girl away from the water.

She staggered back, falling against a passer-by. He turned on Claude: 'Here, what you up to, mate? What's the matter with you?'

Claude brushed him aside, but Laurence had seized the moment and was gone, weaving her way through the crowd with the child in her arms. He followed as best he could, but he was unable to keep up with her. She was swallowed up by the great mass of people.

He worked his way back towards the centre of the town. He must find a policeman, get help; but what help would that be? Until someone from the village picked up his message and followed him here, there was no one else who would recognize Chiara and the girl in a crowd.

He stopped for a moment to rest. His leg was beginning to hurt like hell; this was just the kind of thing that his doctors had warned him not to do. He leaned on the railing at the edge of the promenade and looked across the river; and there, on the opposite bank, he saw Laurence and Chiara.

There were fewer people on that side of the river; it was easy to pick them out. The girl was standing right at the water's edge, with Chiara beside her, trustingly clasping her hand. He saw, with dreadful clarity, what was about to happen, and yelled out: 'Laurence! No!'

His voice echoed across the narrow valley, between the high white cliffs. People turned and stared, but the girl seemed hardly to have heard him. In what seemed like horrifying slow motion, she lifted Chiara in her arms, took a step towards the edge, and plunged into the water.

She must have thought it was deeper. There was a moment of anticlimax, black farce, as she stood there looking slightly ridiculous, the water reaching only to her shoulders. And then the swirling undertow swept her off balance. Claude could do nothing but watch, sickened and helpless, as she sank among the tangled weeds, sucked away by the swift green current.

But Chiara, happy little water baby, bobbed on the smooth calm surface, towards the raft of debris by the bank. The water-rat, asleep on the raft, opened its little eyes and stared at her.

'Hamster!' she said; and then the arms of strangers were reaching down to lift her from the water.